Anne Perry is a *New York Times* bestselling aut...
memorable characters, historical accuracy and exp...
social and ethical issues. She has written a multitude of bests...
novels including her highly acclaimed Monk mysteries, Thomas
Pitt and Daniel Pitt novels, and a spy thriller series featuring Elena
Standish. Anne Perry was selected by *The Times* as one of the
twentieth century's '100 Masters of Crime.'

For a complete list of Anne Perry's historical mysteries, including the Monk series and the Pitt series, as well as her many other novels, visit:

www.headline.co.uk
www.anneperry.co.uk

Anne PERRY

A CHRISTMAS RESOLUTION

HEADLINE

First published in 2020 by
HEADLINE PUBLISHING GROUP

First published in paperback in 2021 by
HEADLINE PUBLISHING GROUP

1

Cataloguing in Publication Data is available from the British Library

ISBN 978 1 4722 7510 3

Typeset in Times New Roman PS by
Palimpsest Book Production Limited, Falkirk, Stirlingshire

Printed and bound in Great Britain by Clays Ltd, Elcograf S.p.A.

HEADLINE PUBLISHING GROUP
An Hachette UK Company
Carmelite House
50 Victoria Embankment
London EC4Y 0DZ

www.headline.co.uk
www.hachette.co.uk

To all who, in these most difficult times,
dare to believe.

Celia approached the vicar, where he stood alone for a few moments in the shadow of the rounded arch above the doorway, sheltered from the rising wind. She wanted to say something about the excellence of his sermon that he could believe, not just the usual 'well done', which covered anything and nothing.

'That really was beautiful. You made me hear it again as good news,' she said with a smile. 'I know the message is familiar, but you made me hear it with the weight of meaning that was new. You must know that.' She knew that he did not.

As always at church, everyone was dressed in their Sunday best, women with bonnets and touches of fur, men with hats in their hands, the wealthier of them with rich astrakhan collars to match. And, of course, gloves. Everyone wore gloves. The cold winds blowing up off the Thames seemed to go straight through the layers of even the most expensive winter clothes. But at this moment, the departing congregation were all too spellbound by the vicar to feel the cold, as was Celia.

Normally, the Reverend Arthur Roberson was not a very enthusiastic speaker. He was pleasant enough to look at, mild mannered and with an abundance of grey hair, although he was little over fifty. His voice was clear and well-modulated, and he could sing with power. Usually, his sermons were competent, but not much more. However, today he spoke with an unaccustomed passion. Music filled his voice and his face was alight with the strength of his emotions.

'That is the message of the gospel,' he said to her. 'The meaning of Christmas for all mankind, indeed for all the earth. No one is excluded, from the first year of our Lord until this year of grace 1872. And always, there is repentance for any and all sins. You cannot commit an act, entertain a thought, that God does not know.' He spread his arms wide, his eyes shining. 'You cannot imagine any sin He has not already seen, and forgiven, if only you repent. From the small everyday sins of thoughtlessness, not caring about the grief of others, all the pain done by indifference,' he shook his head, 'all the way to the depths of violence or depravity that lie at the edge of nightmare, it is all reachable to God. Such is His mercy and understanding.'

A man was approaching them, speaking to no one until he stood almost at the vicar's elbow where he could not be ignored. Seth Marlowe was a prominent member of the congregation, an outspoken leader of thought, which he expressed more often than Celia cared for. That was partly because she disliked him, which she was ashamed of, and partly because his opinions sounded to her unnecessarily rigid, unyielding, where she would have seen reason to make exceptions. One should *temper the wind to the shorn lamb*. What one person could disregard, another might find deeply wounding.

She knew Seth Marlowe was a man who had suffered both the death of his wife some years ago now, and the defection of his daughter, their only child. She should try harder to make an exception for him. She told herself that regularly. And another reason to make allowances for him was that he was the vicar's brother-in-law. The vicar's late wife had been his sister, and had also died young, leaving such wildly different men to grieve for their wives. The two women had also died very differently: Una Roberson of tuberculosis, slowly and with varying degrees of pain, but she was deeply loved, and died in her own home. The vicar still mourned for her quietly but had filled his life with carrying out his duties, ministering to the whole village with gentleness. To Celia, it sometimes looked like overindulgence or, to put it less kindly, weakness. Then she was ashamed of the thought. She did not know the secrets of other people's feelings: guilt, abandonment, hopelessness, loneliness, or even the fear that there was no justice, no forgiveness and no love in the world.

Rose Marlowe, on the other hand – at least according to her husband, Seth – had left home, abandoning him and their only child, and run off to God only knew where. Her father believed she was living on the streets. Rose had eventually died, almost definitely by her own hand, leaving Seth haunted by a different kind of grief, and a source of anger that never left him.

Now, Seth Marlowe was very clearly wanting to speak to the vicar and was not going to wait much longer.

Celia reminded herself that she had never walked

Seth Marlowe's path of betrayal and grief. She knew she should be kinder. Not only to try to understand, but to acknowledge that she didn't understand: also, to exercise less judgement and show more kindness. But she could not like him, and she liked herself the less because of that.

'Good morning, Mr Marlowe,' Celia said, forcing a smile. 'Wasn't it an outstanding sermon? I'm sure everyone benefited from it, and will go away the richer.'

'I hope they will also go away better. After all, a good sermon is a great deal more than comforting, Miss …' he corrected himself, '… Mrs Hooper. It is the true meaning of Christmas, which is too often overlooked in festivities.' He turned to the vicar, excluding Celia in a gesture. 'Arthur, if I might have a word with you? I have something to tell you of importance.'

'Of course,' the vicar replied. He always listened to anyone, no matter what they had to say.

Celia wondered if he ever lost patience and told them to deal with whatever troubles faced them themselves.

'I wish you to be the first to know,' Marlowe said with a freezing glance at Celia, but she did not move.

He had chosen a public place to interrupt. She was not going to be dismissed by him.

Marlowe gave something close to a smile. 'I am going to be married to Clementine Appleby. As soon as it can be arranged in all decency.'

He went on talking, but Celia froze. Clementine was perhaps Celia's closest friend in this village by the Thames, a stone's throw away from London itself. Clementine was a little over thirty, old for a woman marrying for the first time, and from her own bitter experience of loneliness and exclusion, Celia understood Clementine well. Celia was just over forty, and less than a year ago married a man with whom she was deeply in love. It was a happiness she wished for everyone, especially Clementine, who, like herself, had no close family. But to be marrying Seth Marlowe? That bitter, cruel man. She couldn't!

Marlowe was staring at her now, his eyes critical. 'Are you not happy for me, Mrs Hooper? And for your friend Clementine? She will have a social position beyond yours, since your husband is a … dock labourer, or something of the sort …'

'He is a senior officer in the Thames River Police,' she snapped. She wanted to add that she had married for love, not social position, but that would be petty, and imply something of Clementine that she did not for a moment believe. Yet it could hardly be for love that she was marrying Marlowe.

Marlowe stared at her with a smirk.

Celia drew in her breath to say something kinder, but Roberson spoke before her.

'God is not a respecter of persons, Seth. Many of the greatest spirits come in the humblest form. You should not forget that. I think Clementine is one of them. You are very fortunate, and I trust you will care for her, and make her happiness your greatest aim.' There was a pinched look in his face, a hollowness. Did he feel as shocked as Celia did, even afraid?

'I should like to discuss arrangements with you,' Marlowe said to the vicar. 'Privately, if you please.' He shot another cold look at Celia. 'I do not wish Mrs Hooper to participate. She is a bad influence on Clementine. She has … I do not wish to be unkind … unsuitable ideas about quite a lot of things.' He raised his voice slightly to be heard by others. 'And has been mentioned in the newspapers.' He gave a sour smile. 'Not the society pages, but court reports on crime. I will say no more, but I hope you understand, Arthur, that part of my duty towards the woman who will be my wife is to protect her from undesirable influences, and from scandal.'

Celia felt as if she had been struck in the face. She was almost robbed of breath. She knew exactly what Marlowe was referring to, of course.

It was a case about a year ago in which she had met John Hooper, who was an investigating policeman in the biggest horror and tragedy in her life, the kidnapping and murder of her beloved cousin, Katherine. Katherine's husband, Harry Exeter, had been accused of killing his wife and also a woman prepared to give testimony against him. During that time, Celia had fallen in love with Hooper. When Exeter had found out about Hooper's earlier life as a seaman, and how he had led the crew against a captain who had miscalculated the ship's position and had very nearly driven the vessel on to a reef, which would have torn the hull open and resulted in the drowning of every man on board, he used that to force Celia to give him an alibi. It didn't matter to him that Hooper had saved all the crew's lives, and to some extent the captain's reputation. The only thing Exeter wanted was to walk free of two murders. If she lied, then Hooper's secret would be kept. On the other hand, if she spoke what she knew, then

Exeter would hang, but he would make damned sure that Hooper did too. Because what Hooper had done to save lives had been a form of mutiny, which was a capital crime. Even if he, by some miracle, escaped the noose, he would certainly lose his job with the River Police. Celia had done the only thing she could: she had lied on the witness stand.

Details of the case had been printed in the worst of the newspapers. They had made a very big thing of the fact that her obvious love for Hooper had driven her to commit perjury. The papers had omitted to say that she had been pardoned by the judge and never charged with anything.

Standing outside the church now, staring at Marlowe as if mesmerised, her face burning, Celia felt all the misery and fear of that time over-whelming her. She had never told Arthur Roberson about it – not that this omission disturbed her. It was the humiliation of having been exposed to the public as a woman so in love with a man who had made no advances towards her that she would do such a thing for him. It had sounded so desperate … and pathetic.

Both men were staring at her now.

It was Roberson who spoke first. 'I am surprised

that you read such newspapers, Seth. Muckraking. I had thought better of you. If you had chosen *The Times*, it would have told you that Exeter was found guilty, and of the superb work of the River Police in investigating the case, and the terrible death of Katherine Exeter—'

'You never would face the truth about people, Arthur,' Marlowe returned. 'You put women on a pedestal. Foolish. When they fall off, as they inevitably will, then they break more than their own reputations; they break other people's hearts, and too often their spirits.'

Roberson was speechless for a moment, overwhelmed by too many emotions.

'Nevertheless,' Marlowe went on, 'you will not involve Mrs Hooper in any of my affairs. Is that clear?' He did not wait for an answer. He turned on his heel and strode away.

Celia took a deep breath. 'I don't think he understood your message about forgiveness, Arthur.' She fought back tears and even managed a slight smile, before turning away and beginning to walk home.

She was halfway up the slight incline of the road towards her house and looking forward to the warmth of it, the sweet familiarity, when she heard footsteps behind her. She was in no mood for conversation, and the wind coming up off the river was knife edged, finding every piece of her uncovered skin. She stopped and turned round just as Clementine Appleby reached her. Her eyes were shining and her fair skin was made pink by the wind. Perhaps she was not beautiful, and she definitely was on the wrong side of thirty, but she had a warmth that set her apart. Celia liked her quick humour and her joy in unexpected things: ducklings with little warm, flat feet: wreaths of mist on the river in the early morning light; crisp pancakes with lemon juice; the choice of a pink blouse when one might have expected the predictability of white.

'I tried to catch you,' Clementine said, breathing in deeply. 'Celia, I'm so happy! I can't tell you everything just yet, but I simply had to tell you this. You always understand; you are just about the best friend I have ever had. I wish I could tell my mother.' For a moment her eyes misted over, then she controlled herself and blinked rapidly. She hardly ever mentioned any family, and Celia realised it was not a subject she could speak of. She had no brothers or sisters, and her mother had apparently died some time ago. Celia choked down her own feelings and forced herself to smile.

'Would you like to come home for a cup of tea?' she offered. 'The wind is cruel on this rise; I suppose it's the price we pay for the view.' She gazed beyond Clementine to the wide stretch of the water shining in the icy light, dotted with ships, barges, ferries and occasionally pleasure boats, even in this season.

'May I? That would be lovely, but won't your husband be expecting his Sunday lunch?' Clementine asked hesitantly. She was always loath to intrude.

'Not yet,' Celia promised her. 'He's on duty.'

'It's hard work in the River Police, isn't it?'

'Yes.' Celia said it with pride. She was learning all the time what patience his work required: hardship and long hours in the water, in all weathers, and knowledge of winds and tides and of all manner of men, ships, cargoes, weapons, and the tragedies to be dealt with. She was in awe of his quiet strength, of spirit even more than of body.

Clementine took a quick breath. 'Celia, I am to be married!' Now the words burst from her, too big to be retained any more or alluded to obliquely.

Celia looked at her friend's shining eyes, the smile she could not control. She knew something of the dreams that were hidden behind her protective cheerfulness, and much of it not long ago had been true of herself as well. Celia had married long after she had given up hope of ever having the safety, the dignity, the acceptance of marriage. Perhaps most of all, the belonging. Love was another thing, a dream in itself. Celia had found them all and was savouring the strangeness, the excitement. She was still new to this. Of course, there were things hard to get used to: the lack of privacy at times, the need to bend, to change quite often, to keep opinions to herself. But it was wonderful.

Instinctively, she put her arms around Clementine and hugged her, feeling her relax and return the embrace. 'Wonderful!' she said heartily, stepping back a little. 'I think I am nearly as happy for you as you are yourself. You have been so discreet; I really did not know.' Secretly, in her heart, she wished it were the vicar Clementine was going to wed. He was so terribly lonely and, in spite of the difference in their ages, she would be the perfect wife for him. The whole congregation would rejoice! But she must not let Clementine know that. Her smile must look real, surprised and happy.

Clementine looked back at her, ignoring the

freezing wind. 'Seth Marlowe,' she said. 'He's such a good man; I just hope I can make him happy, after all the grief he's been through.'

Celia was cold to the bone, as if all the layers of protective clothing had been torn from her, leaving her skin naked to the knives of the wind.

Clementine waited.

Celia's mind raced. She must be kind. She must not hurt this girl. Damn Seth Marlowe! 'I had no idea.' That was stupid, she told herself. Say something good about him.

'Don't you think I will make him happy?' Clementine asked. 'You don't think I can keep up to his high standards?' There was a shadow across her face, in her eyes.

Celia did not know what to say, and she knew Clementine had seen it already.

'I am not of his social class,' Clementine added. 'I know that. But I can learn. I can, Celia, I can learn.'

'What on earth makes you think that?' Celia was shocked. Then, like a wave of memory came scores of little things that Clementine had said about her background, her lack of education, her lack of status. Celia had considered it so unimportant as to who she was, and had never followed through with questions. 'Clementine?'

Clementine's face was red with embarrassment, so different from the pleasure she had shown moments ago.

'Clementine? What did your father do? What was his work?' She knew that was the standard by which people were apt to judge, however little it had to do with a person's real worth.

'I don't know,' Clementine said in little more than a whisper. She looked down at the pavement, avoiding Celia's eyes.

'You don't …' Celia began, then the truth struck her almost like a physical blow. 'You don't know who he was!' She gripped Clementine's arms tightly, almost as if she were holding her up.

'No.' The word was little more than a sigh.

'And your mother raised you?' Celia asked.

'Yes.' Clementine held her head high, her eyes defiant. 'She gave me everything she could, she loved me, taught me, protected me …' The wind pulled a little of her hair loose, and she ignored it.

'You don't need to tell me that,' Celia replied with certainty. 'I can see it in everything you are, you say and you do. I am far more concerned that Seth Marlowe is not good enough for you.' This she meant as a bitter truth. If he hurt Clementine, that would be a sin for which God might forgive him, but Celia would not.

'He is a very good man,' Clementine protested. 'When you get to know him better, you will understand that. There is a purity in him that I must try hard to live up to. You will help me, won't you?'

'Of course I will,' Celia promised. It was the only possible answer to give. 'Every step of the way,' she added. 'Now we have to plan what your wedding dress will be like.'

'Not expensive, but graceful,' Clementine said with gravity, then a sudden, shy smile.

'We will all help,' Celia promised. 'Everyone will be happy for you. Every woman in the congregation.'

'Do you think so?'

'Yes! Except, of course, those who are envious.' If she was going to lie, she should go all the way.

Clementine smiled and the sparkle came back into her eyes. 'I knew you'd be happy for me. You don't mind if I go home now, do you? I just wanted to tell you …'

'Of course not!' Celia replied instantly. She meant it. She needed to be alone to absorb this news.

*

Celia ate a light lunch alone at the small table in the kitchen. She would cook a hot dinner to share with Hooper when he returned, probably well after dark. He would be tired after a long day on the river, and no doubt cold, although he did not seem to feel it as much as she did. Or perhaps he was inured to physical hardship by the years he had spent at sea, earlier in his life. She had no idea how anybody would choose such a hard and dangerous occupation, except from the necessity to provide for himself, and perhaps for others. She shuddered to think that maybe that had been what it was: an escape from the bitterest poverty to the alternative dangers of the sea.

One night, when she was warm and safe in bed, lying close to him, hearing his even breathing, she had asked him. He was not a talkative man, but that night he had spoken at length. He had described the beauty of being out at sea; the light in the sky when it seemed to be all around you, the immensity of it from horizon to horizon, and out for ever, beyond the imagination; the stars blazing in the darkness when there was no moon to outshine them, no city light or fog to lessen their glory. 'You feel as if you could reach out and touch them with your hand,' he had said. 'You think of God, who made them, all of

17

them, far more than a man could count in a lifetime, even if he did nothing else.'

She had understood the depth of his words, their magnitude. 'Perhaps we should all see that, at least once,' she had suggested. 'Makes our self-importance look a little absurd. Do you suppose God has a sense of humour?'

He had tightened his arm around her. 'He has to! And perhaps He laughs or cries over us.'

'Do you ever want to go back to sea?' she asked and then, the instant later, wished she had not. She had no right to. And perhaps she did not want the answer.

'Would you come with me?' He touched her hair gently, as if he loved the feel of it through his fingers.

'I would be terrified, but I would,' she said honestly. 'It would be better than being left behind … without you.'

'I've seen some wonderful things,' he said softly. 'I'll tell you about them.'

And he had, little by little, since that night. He had used simple language, but his love of the beauty and the awe came through his words. She smiled now, even at the thought.

*

That Sunday afternoon, Clementine did what she had done for several years now – not every Sunday, but at least two or three a month. She went to visit a refuge for women who were sick, hungry, or homeless, and often who were prostitutes. She had first gone there years ago with her aunt Lily, a good-hearted woman who quietly did what so many others talked about: cared for the less fortunate. When Lily died, Clementine had continued her work. It gave her a quiet, peaceful sense of gratitude for all she had, and a willingness to share it with others.

She packed up some cakes and tarts that she had baked, and, putting on her heaviest cape, went out into the wind. She took the ferry over the river that was a barrier dividing where she lived from where she visited the women. She kept this part of her life a secret because she did not want people to think she was boastful or self-righteous.

It was a bitterly cold journey across the open water, but she loved the winter light, and she knew most of the ferrymen and had heard stories about their experiences.

When she reached the other side, she paid the fare and then went up the steps and along the street, hurrying in the cold, eager to get there and share the cakes. She went into the building and greeted all the people she knew, and then those she did not yet know. She handed out the cakes and pastries – not food for hungry people, just a gesture that they were remembered and she had taken trouble. After all, it was Christmas and weren't they here to sing carols together?

There was a girl she liked particularly. She was about eighteen or nineteen, new to prostitution a couple of years ago. She had tried hard to make a living at regular work, but lost too many jobs through illness, occasionally drinking a little too much, and too often being insolent. She was very pretty, with dark blue eyes and thick, curling auburn hair. Her name was Bessie.

Clementine was eager to talk to her, and when her basket of baked goods was empty she went over and sat beside her. They talked about trivial things. It was not the subject that mattered, it was the tone of voice, the smile, the full attention given to the girl by somebody who liked her and didn't want anything in return.

'You look happy,' Bessie said, watching Clementine's face. 'You're expecting a good Christmas? You've got family?' She looked away, as if she did not want Clementine to read the loneliness in her eyes.

'No,' Clementine answered. 'But I will have soon. I'm going to be married.'

'What's he like?' Bessie asked, turning back to face her.

'He's quite a lot older than I am,' Clementine replied. 'But he's … a very good man.'

'It's all that matters,' Bessie said candidly. 'It makes up for everything else.'

'I think so, too,' Clementine agreed. 'He's honest, prudent, very … I don't know. It's hard to describe. He's always fair. Everybody respects him.' She tried to say what it was about Seth Marlowe that she liked. 'I know I can trust him.' She smiled. 'He's been badly hurt in the past. I want to make him happy again.'

'You will,' Bessie replied with certainty. 'You'd make anybody happy … if you wanted to.' There was a faraway, wistful look in her eyes. 'What's his name?'

'Seth Marlowe,' Clementine replied.

Bessie sat perfectly still. She hardly seemed even to breathe.

'Bessie?' Clementine put one hand on the girl's arm.

'Oh! Sorry. I was … daydreaming.' She turned to look at Clementine. 'Does he live near where you do? You moving to his house or is he moving to yours?'

'I don't have a house,' Clementine admitted. 'I just lodge with an old lady, and look after her. Do the cooking, cleaning and all that.'

'So where will you live then?' Bessie's eyes filled with tears. 'I suppose it means you won't be coming here any more.' She wiped the tears away angrily.

'No, it doesn't,' Clementine said quickly. Seth would approve of her coming to visit such people and giving whatever help she could. She gave Bessie a description of Miss Drew's house, and then of Seth's house, and then something of the whole village.

'Sounds nice,' Bessie said, making herself smile, but not looking at Clementine. 'You will come again, won't you?'

'Definitely,' Clementine promised. 'I might bring a friend.' She thought of Celia. If Seth were displeased with her for going to such a place alone, Celia would come with her, she knew that. 'You'll like her, too, and she'll like you,' she added.

When the other women were gathered together, Bessie said to Clementine, 'Are you going to sing with us?' She stood up and walked slowly up to the others, until they were all in a group. Clementine joined them and the music began. It was an old piano, and some of the notes were missing, but the sweetness of the singing made up for it.

Celia made hot stew with thought and care. It was the sort of thing that would not spoil, were it served an hour or two later than planned. She was getting good at that, and it gave her pleasure to see her husband's enjoyment of it. Her ... husband.

Hooper was tired and cold when he finally came home. He took off his heavy pea coat and his boots, washed at the basin, and then sat down to eat.

They spoke of trivial things, and then ate in companionable silence in the small room full of books. His precious few had been read many times in lonely hours at sea. There were some surprising classics among them, even slim volumes of poetry whose words could be read time and time again without growing stale. And books of hers: Jane Austen and the Brontë sisters, plus books on history, gardening, the dreams and memories of many people in the past whose inner thoughts were anything but pedestrian. Celia found their company timeless.

Where this room once felt bare, it was now pleasantly crowded with memories and hopes.

Celia served a fresh apple pie with a little cream. After the meal, Hooper sat by the fire while she cleared the table.

A few minutes passed, then he leaned over, added another log of wood, then sat back again in his chair, looking at her. 'What is it?' he asked. His tone did not change; it was still casual, as if he were continuing a conversation already begun.

The knot inside her tightened. She still had not made up her mind on how much to tell him about Clementine, but the moment had come when she had to answer, or make it an evasion he would recognise. Would it hurt him? It would hurt her, if it were the other way around.

He waited, his eyes searching her face.

'I learned a lot more about Clementine today,' she began.

He frowned. 'Bad things?'

'Oh, no. I mean, not anything bad that she has done.' Now she must explain, or he would not believe her. 'I learned that she has no father.'

As usual, he was direct. 'You mean she's illegitimate. So are a lot of people. Does it matter to you?'

She was horrified. 'No, of course not!' She was hurt that he could even consider this. 'It means she is far more vulnerable than most of us, that she had no man in her life in her growing-up years for her to …'

He waited.

'… to know how she should be treated,' she finished.

'Celia, what has really changed today? Clementine has known this for years. What is it you are afraid of?'

He was never evasive, at least not with her. She answered just as bluntly. 'She told me she is going to marry Seth Marlowe.' Then she looked at him. The disapproval was immediately clear in his eyes. 'I had to pretend to be pleased for her. She needs it so much.' Would he understand that for a man to be unmarried was no shame, but to be an unmarried woman? That meant no one would have you. She had felt the steady, angry pain of that tighten within her, and she was ready to defend Clementine.

'Well, it can't be because she is with child,' he said with a twisted smile she misunderstood.

'Why not?' she challenged him. 'She's not so old that she couldn't be, John. She's only just over thirty.' She felt the double sting of that: she herself was almost certainly too old for childbearing.

'Not with that passionless husk of a man,' he replied. 'With someone else, quite possibly.'

She thought of Clementine's shining eyes, filled with hope, and found her own eyes welling with tears.

'And you are afraid for her?' Hooper asked. 'That little by little he will kill her spirit?'

She looked up. 'Yes, I think I am, and I hate myself for it. The whole sermon today was about repentance and forgiveness. It was the best sermon I have ever heard Arthur Roberson give. I think everyone believed that. It was as if we emerged from the church in a wave of joy, and it wasn't just hope. What he said was true, it made sense, and it was for every man and woman on earth.' She reached for his hand. 'John, why am I so mean-spirited that I can't be glad, and hope for Marlowe that Clementine will bring him happiness at last?'

He smiled, looked down at their hands clasped together on her knee, then up again. He was not a handsome man – his face was weathered by years at sea – but there was a great gentleness in it. 'You can hope,' he replied. 'But you have more sense than to think it is likely. I admire your faith in God, and I'm trying to learn from it, but you never believed that it would all be easy. What would we learn from that?'

'He's already suffered a great deal,' she pointed out. 'His first wife, Rose, brought him nothing but grief and shame. Doesn't he deserve a little happiness?'

'I don't think deserving has anything to do with it,' Hooper said thoughtfully. 'But if you think he does deserve it, why are you so upset now?'

She looked away. 'Because I don't like him. I think he's self-righteous and judgemental. And he'll hurt Clementine, probably convinced all the time that he's making her a better woman, which he will interpret as more submissive, more obedient and more grateful.'

He laughed outright, a rich, joyous sound she heard too seldom. His job was hard, and he saw too much tragedy. He felt it, even if he seldom allowed anyone else to see it. The reward lay in the fellowship of the men he worked with, and the knowledge that he was making the river, called by some 'the longest street in London', a better place.

'Are you laughing at me?' she asked without resentment.

'I love you,' he said simply. 'Keep your own

wisdom. Don't let the world's wisdom, with its hard experiences, overtake you. It isn't always right.'

The warmth spread through her. All those years alone, fending for herself, and now this: a man who not only loved her, but respected her. 'I hope not. It's often so dark. But I still feel guilty for listening with a whole heart to the vicar's sermon, knowing he was right. What he said was beautiful and true, and yet, less than half an hour later, I was horrified that Clementine was thinking of marrying Marlowe. I was filled with fear and anger, real anger.' She smiled ruefully. 'I wanted God to forgive everyone, including me, even Seth Marlowe, but just don't let him marry Clementine!' She looked steadily into Hooper's face. Then drew in a sharp breath. 'Oh God, that means I haven't really forgiven him, doesn't it? And that I still don't want him to have happiness, acceptance, to belong again – at least not to Clementine. I really believe he will hurt her. Not physically, of course, but emotionally.' She took a deep breath. 'When you love someone, you care desperately what they think of you.' It was a confession of her own vulnerability. It would hurt beyond bearing if Hooper were truly disappointed in her.

'I know,' he said in little above a whisper. 'That's

the best and the worst of caring so much. That's why we need the ordinary things, just to make it bearable, a common cause that matters, but where failure is bearable. You get up and try again.' He gave a half-smile, very gently. 'You forgive the other person, and you forgive yourself.'

'I've got to be sorry first, though, haven't I?' It was only half a question. There was only one answer.

'Yes,' he agreed. 'But you don't have to like him.'

'Good, because I don't think I can. I feel such a hypocrite. Everyone can forgive the people they like. Just shrug it off and the next day you don't even remember it. You don't want to, so it slips away, and we're happy to let it, so it's easy.'

'And did the Reverend Mr Roberson say that?' he asked.

'Say what?'

'That it's easy to forgive those you like? That is the test, isn't it … forgiving those you don't like? Especially those who have hurt someone you love. Anyone can do the easy things.'

She knew exactly what he meant, and he was right. 'I'm a hypocrite,' she admitted.

He leaned forward and kissed her on the lips softly

and infinitely gently. She felt happiness fill her, a warmth flooding her whole body. This was unforgivable. She was far too happy to dare deny anyone else all the joy they could find. She must truly stop judging Seth Marlowe. Dislike him all you want, she told herself, but don't dare judge him. She raised her hand and touched Hooper's face softly, tenderly, and let this happiness take over all her thoughts.

Hooper went to work early next morning, just before sunrise. So close to Christmas, it was nearly the shortest day of the year. A heavy mist clung to the face of the river, scattering the sheen on the water and veiling the wharfs and warehouses, the closely moored ships in grey. Only the plain black lines of the spars were visible.

He found it beautiful. Perhaps that was eccentric, but he watched the faint breeze stirring the vapour like a slow breathing, each moment revealing a little more: a black mast drawing circles in the sky as the tide moved the hull of a ship riding at anchor; flashes of silver light, slow-crawling ferries criss-crossing the surface like long-legged beetles, as if their oars were holding them up on the water.

He missed the endless horizon of being at sea, but

he still found the solitude, the vagaries of the weather, the moods and the thin threat of danger beneath the safety of the settling fog, at this time of the year, almost every night. And now there was this unbelievable happiness of being with Celia. He had only just realised that he could love another person, spend all his spare time with her, share many of his thoughts, and not feel as if he had lost his freedom or his individuality.

Of course, there were difficult moments, but they were of no importance at all. She never intruded. Why was that? Was she afraid to? In case he minded? She was so vulnerable in completely surprising ways: she could be hurt more than he had realised was possible by a careless word, or silence where there should have been something said, at least an acknowledgement. How could that hurt? It was never the gesture she minded; it was the omission.

And she was shy about certain things. He liked that. It made him acutely conscious of the difference between a man and a woman. It was at once exciting and infinitely tender, and he wondered how he had ever waited so long even to seek marriage – except the answer was obvious: he was a solitary man. Only

Celia, with her quiet grace, her sublime courage, was right for him.

They had met quite by chance, on a very terrible case of kidnap, and one of the most appalling murders he had ever seen – and he had seen his share. The river was a dangerous place. People came from every corner of the earth, every continent and island, every ocean and clime. The Pool of London was the busiest dockland in the world, the heart of an empire that spanned the globe. And all the violence and greed that it engendered. Yet the Exeter murder was still one of the worst.

Sometimes he sat in the small house, her house and now theirs, watched her in the kitchen, and thought of her in the witness stand ... and the lie she had told to save him, even knowing the truth about his life at sea, and saying nothing. She had done it partly for him, but also because she would not see an injustice done, no matter what it cost her. Quietly, in her own way, unperceived and unacknowledged, she was one of the bravest people he had ever known.

And she was funny and gentle, wise and eccentric. Hooper knew why she did some of the things she did, but he refrained from commenting. It made her unusual, a mystery sometimes, but never a bore.

He was concerned for her now, and the hurt he might cause her. He had not said so, but he had met Seth Marlowe only half a dozen times and he did not like the man. Hooper had learned that few people's lives were as they seemed at a glance. If they were, if there were no painful secrets, no complex motives behind even the simplest actions, no loves or hates that bent memories and judgements, there would be no need for detecting skills and the River Police – or any other police, for that matter. Not much was as simple as it appeared at a glance. It was seldom a case of innocent or guilty; more often it was a matter of degree.

He thought again of the Exeter case and how he had met Celia. Nothing was the way it seemed at first. It was like the mud in the sinking slum of Jacob's Island, and how it had changed, shifted on its foundation, a fraction with every tide, always a little lower. More menacing.

He walked more briskly. He would catch a ferry at the next stairs down to the water, and then on to Wapping and the police station there. It was time to put all personal issues aside. Seth Marlowe was not a likeable man, but other than his effect on Celia, Hooper was too full of his own happiness to wish him ill. If Clementine brought him any joy at all, he could only be better for it.

It was on the Thursday of that week when Celia went into the church with her armful of flowers, although they were mostly leaves and berries. As winter deepened, leaves were fallen and there were few flowers. She had several sprays of holly. It was a shame to cut them, but the bush nearest her front door was enormous and could do with a trimming. And really, there was so little else. Laurel was green, but it always reminded her of wreaths, albeit for victory rather than death. But the symbolism was a little heavy. She had gathered half a dozen late chrysanthemums of a lovely tawny gold, but apart from these there was only hellebore, a beautiful flower in quite a variety of colours: white, yellow, pink, purples and green. They grew best in the shade and always reminded her of mourning. Perhaps it was the colours. Today, she had cut the purple ones, and those touched with pink.

She put them down on the bench in the chilly side room kept for such chores. There was always a pair of secateurs there, and of course the vases, and a small sink with a cold-water tap. It was a pleasant task, and she looked forward to it. She enjoyed the challenge of trying to make the bouquets look rich, joyous, as if from an abundance. She disliked too much ribbon, which made a very obvious mark of the scarcity of flowers.

She was about halfway through when she heard footsteps behind her. She did not expect the vicar, but she would have been pleased enough to see him. She turned round and froze. It was not the Reverend Mr Roberson who stood a short distance from her, but Seth Marlowe. He was dressed in a well-tailored business suit of dark wool, and carried his hat in one hand. He smiled, but it was gone in an instant, as if it were a bleak formality.

'Good morning, Mrs Hooper. I thought I should find you here. You are something of a creature of habit.'

She was surprised. His words made it clear that he had come specifically to see her, and there was nothing of chance in the encounter. It was a little chilling to think she was so predictable, and that he knew it. She felt immediately defensive.

'A creature of habit.' She could hear the irritation in her own voice. 'I would prefer to think of myself as reliable, someone who keeps my word. From your frequently expressed opinions on vice and virtue, I would have thought you might appreciate that.'

'I do, Mrs Hooper, if not finding reliability very interesting,' he replied. 'It is bare minimum of what one would expect.'

Celia put the last chrysanthemum in the place she had chosen for it, then turned back to face him again. 'I cannot believe your life is so devoid of things to do that you came all the way here to tell me that.' She nearly added more, then realised it would give away that she was angry. So, she stood silently, waiting for him to explain. Her earlier good intentions had entirely evaporated.

'Of course not!' he snapped. 'I've come for a very specific purpose, at a time when I would be able to have a confidential talk with you. You and I do not approve of each other nor, indeed, like each other.' He waved his hand as if brushing away crumbs. 'But that is of no importance. I think you are a meddle-some and rather tedious woman. No doubt you think that I am over-strict in my judgements, and you are jealous of the esteem in which the vicar holds my opinions.' He gave a slight shrug. 'I appreciate that you have been of considerable support to him at the time of his bereavement. I suppose you were of reasonable assistance, though, as you observed on Sunday, he had no notion of your ... actions, and reputation ...'

She looked straight at Marlowe, standing too close to her in the small room. Her eyes were level, not for a second wavering. 'Think what you wish, Mr Marlowe. If you imagine I care in the slightest what that is, you are mistaken. I married for love, not out of desperation. I hope you can say the same. Clementine deserves a great deal more than filling a blank space in your life. I can't help wondering if you need someone to fill it, and perhaps anyone will do.'

It was his turn to blush, but it looked more out of anger than embarrassment. He took a half-step towards her. 'I came here to warn you to mind your own business regarding my marriage to Miss Appleby. Or any other of my business, for that matter. Stick to arranging flowers, Mrs Hooper, and laundering the linen. Clementine seems to find a mother figure in you, or perhaps an aunt would be more accurate.'

Celia raised her eyebrows. 'And what else is it you imagine I might do that apparently worries you so much?'

'Gossip, Mrs Hooper. Advice that she does not

need, and that you have no right to offer,' he replied immediately.

Celia raised her eyebrows. 'Really, I find it offensive, Mr Marlowe, that you would restrict a woman you purport to love from asking advice from other women, on matters that may be personal, and about which you can know nothing. Even though, as we are all aware, you have been married before.' She knew that would sting. He had spoken of his first wife, and referred with anger and grief to her many failings. His pain at her shame, humiliation and total fall from grace was an agony that burst out of him like internal bleeding, momentarily out of control. It awakened pity and embarrassment, a memory no one wanted, of how disastrously far the highest hopes could fall and that, like a plague disease, it could strike anyone, even the most righteous, which Seth Marlowe certainly believed he was.

'I think your experience of marriage is very slight, Mrs Hooper.' There was a definite sneer on his face.

'You mean very recent,' she corrected him. 'And perhaps the more helpful for that. But I am happy for Clementine.' That was a lie that burned her tongue. She was terrified for her. 'And I shall be happy to give her any advice she wishes.'

'I have asked you courteously, Mrs Hooper,' he answered stiffly. 'If you do not give me the respect of obeying my wishes, then—'

'Obeying?' Celia interrupted incredulously.

'Certainly, obeying. Clementine is to be my wife.'

'If she wishes to *obey* you, that is her choice,' Celia said coldly. 'I am not your wife, nor of any other relationship to you, and I should do what I think right.'

'Your husband will teach you in time,' he answered, 'if he is man enough. If not, he will come to live with the consequences.' He did not conceal a slight smile. 'I presume you wish him to be happy, and to retain your … status.'

Celia felt the first real chill run through her. If this was how Clementine's marriage began, how would it continue? Love, honour and obey – suddenly the words took on a darker meaning. She had made that exact vow herself, thinking only of advice, of wishes, never of any type of force.

Marlowe was watching her closely. She realised for the first time that his eyes were pale grey, like stones.

'I perceive you are beginning to understand,' he said with the slightest of smiles. 'You will not give

Clementine advice, except on such things as how to dress for the wedding, and on personal matters of …' He shrugged and let the sentence hang in the air, as if it did not need finishing. The thought was too delicate to be given words.

'I should give Clementine advice as she asks for it,' Celia stated flatly. It was an insufficient answer, but she had nothing better.

Marlowe stood quite still, looking past her to the magnificent urn she had arranged of mostly leaves, but with splashes of the glorious chrysanthemum colour.

'Impulsive,' he said, as if the word carried a wealth of meaning too heavy and too subtle for defining, but understood between them.

Celia could think of no reply.

'The quality that can lead you into a world of error, for which you might pay dearly.' He smiled, but it was an expression she did not know how to read.

'Is that a threat, Mr Marlowe? Are you saying that if I give Clementine any advice you do not agree with, you will hurt her? Or that somehow or other you will hurt me?' She said it incredulously, and in truth it was almost unbelievable.

His eyebrows rose. 'You will hurt yourself, Mrs

Hooper. If your behaviour is less than she thinks worthy of you, then she would be bitterly hurt. She is young, generous-hearted, but she judges rashly; indeed, sometimes not at all.'

'Qualities for which she is both loved and admired, Mr Marlowe. I would think by you most of all.'

'Generosity is very charming, particularly in those who are most in need of it, but in the end, the truth remains,' he answered, looking a little past her at the bench with its cut stalks and leaves sitting by the secateurs. He frowned, as if at the untidiness of it.

'Were you not listening on Sunday, Mr Marlowe?' Now there was a very hard edge to Celia's voice. 'The burden of the vicar's sermon was that there is forgiveness. Did you did not hear that?'

He looked back at her. 'After repentance, Mrs Hooper. I fear that it is you who are hearing the message selectively.'

'And I should repent of giving Clementine such advice as she might ask for? I assume you will know this by cross-questioning her as to our private conversations between women.'

His expression was bitter. 'I am sorry you forced me to say this, but I was not referring to future impulsiveness you might indulge, but to the past.'

She knew what he was talking about: the Exeter case. She did not think of herself as emotional, and certainly not impulsive. In fact, others had said she was dull, even at times rather boring. She had never been told how deep her feelings were, but at that moment in court, she had let the world see the depth of her passion.

'The trial of Harry Exeter,' Marlowe said softly. He was looking straight at her now, unblinking. 'You swore, in the name of God, and told a deliberate lie. Not a minor one, due to confusion, or lapse of memory, but a deliberate lie, for your own emotional reasons.'

The tide of heat rose, burning up her skin. 'I do not read the gutter press, as apparently you do, Mr Marlowe. And I imagine you will not allow Clementine access to such things.'

'It is pointless to lie, Mrs Hooper,' Marlowe went on. 'Your guilt is scarlet in your face.'

She scrambled desperately for something to say, any defence at all. But she could think of nothing to silence him. He had no right to know! How he must hate her to do this. And Clementine – would she even understand why Celia had done the only thing she could think of to see true justice? No, that was

42

less than the truth. All that had filled her mind was that John Hooper would hang for doing something for which he had had no choice. And Harry Exeter, who had murdered Katherine so brutally, would go free. But if she had to do it again, even not knowing that Hooper loved her in return, she would make the same decision.

She faced Marlowe, as if he had been something revolting that had crawled out from under a wet stone. 'You must do as you think right,' she replied. She meant it to sound icy, filled with contempt, but her voice shook too much to have any conviction.

'The vicar will be disappointed,' Marlowe went on, studying her face. 'He thinks so highly of you. He hid it well, but he was appalled to learn of your ... lies. And your husband, complicit in the perjury – and it is perjury, you know – may find his own position in jeopardy.' The smile just touched his lips. 'Has he any other skills, if they choose to dismiss him without honour? He could always become a dock labourer, I suppose.'

'He did not lie.' She managed to force out the words between stiff lips. 'And I was not his wife then, so he had no responsibility for my choices. In fact, he did not know it was a lie.' That was the truth.

'Was that your reward for lying?' he asked, his eyebrows rising again. 'Marriage?'

She found her tongue. 'Is that how you see marriage, as the reward for some otherwise appalling act?' She was surprised at herself, but she did not for one instant wish that she could take it back.

His face drained of all colour and his arm swung back sharply, as if he would strike her. Then he changed his mind and let it fall, fist still clenched.

Celia was almost sorry. If he had hit her, even if not very hard, it would have put him irreparably in the wrong.

'It is you who are at fault, Mrs Hooper,' he said coldly. 'You lied after swearing in God's name to tell the truth. That cannot likely be forgiven, as if it were a slip of the tongue, something done in innocence, or by mistake.'

'No,' she agreed. 'I did it because I believed it was the right thing to do, the lesser of two evils.'

'Oh, really. Please do not expect me to believe that.' His expression was an open sneer.

'I would have expected you to give me the benefit of the doubt, or to overlook it in the circumstances, as the judge did,' she retaliated. 'Or, at least, I would have done, even until last Sunday. Would you have betrayed yourself, Mr Marlowe? Now I expect nothing of you except cruelty and violence. You must be very afraid of something. Perhaps of Clementine finding out what kind of a man you really are.'

'Are you threatening to tell her some vile story about me?' His voice grated. 'Something to dissuade her from marrying me? You will fail. She loves me, and sees a future ahead of her safer and far more respectable than anything in her past. She can hold her head up in the community.'

The shadow of doubt fell upon Celia for an instant, a memory of Clementine standing with a group of women, but a little apart. Was it imaginable that they knew of her birth, of the mother who had raised her so carefully and with such love, but without a father? Could Marlowe know that? And would he tell people? Perhaps carefully, one or two at a time. That would make it impossible for Clementine to discover who knew, and once married to him she could not leave. Was that why his first wife had left? Some calculated cruelty that had robbed her of every other choice?

She forced the words out. 'Yes, she is well liked,' she said, her voice wavering a little. 'Anyone who hurt her would be most unpopular.'

'I'm glad you appreciate that.'

'I do, but I wonder if you do.'

He froze for an instant. Then a slow smile spread across his face. 'You were under oath and you lied. That is a crime. I told her, with regret, that you were an unsuitable person for her to associate with, and unfortunately nothing you say can be taken as the truth.'

Celia stared at him and was certain that he meant exactly what he said. Why? What was he so frightened that she would tell Clementine? Something that could injure him? 'What is it?' she said. 'What are you so dreadfully afraid of that you would stoop to black-mailing me like this? That is despicable.'

His face lost the last vestige of colour, and she knew in that instant that she had made a mistake, and there was no way to take it back. Any kind of a retreat at all would signal fear and vulnerability. This was absurd. She had seen Seth Marlowe almost every Sunday for years, ever since he had come to this area soon after the death of his wife. She had heard about Rose Marlowe from Rose's sister-in-law, Una Roberson, especially in the last months, when Una knew she was dying. She was worried and needed someone to confide in. Celia had tried to comfort her.

'Blackmail is an ugly word, Mrs Hooper,' Marlowe said after a moment's silence. 'I am merely warning you that poor Arthur Roberson thought so well of you that to learn of your perjury would hurt him very deeply. He may not be able to hide it from the congregation. People will wonder what you have done, and speculation is seldom kind. I am sure you understand.'

Thoughts raced through her mind. 'No, it isn't,' she said. 'People speculate about all sorts of things.' She took a breath, as if the room were suffocatingly hot. 'Such as what really happened to your wife or your daughter.'

He stared at her, all expression draining from his face, leaving it haggard, as if he had aged decades as she watched him. 'It was you.' Sudden understanding lit his eyes until they glittered between his narrowed lids. 'Behind that so innocent smile, there is the venom that kills the heart. The one person I never suspected. Well, you will not win. I forbid you to see Clementine, or speak to her again, except in public.'

Celia caught her breath. 'What is it you think I have done?' she demanded.

'Don't play innocent with me, miss. I read it.'

'Read ... what? I don't know what you're talking

about.' Had he taken leave of his senses? 'You make a big noise about how you never drink alcohol, but I think you must be drunk now. You are making no sense and you look crazy.' It was no exaggeration. He was swaying slightly on his feet, and his whole body shook. If she were not so very angry, she would have been frightened of him, even here, inside the church.

'It's too late to pretend innocence,' he said contemptuously. 'You wrote that poisonous letter to me … oh, clever, so clever. Well, I can tell people about you, and I will if you drive me to it, I swear. I don't want to tell Clementine, but I will, so help me God. If you mention the letter to her, I will tell her who wrote it.'

Celia was stunned. Her mind raced, trying to think what he could be talking about. What letter? She wrote very few, and they were only to distant family members, cousins she barely knew. They were Christmas and birthday wishes, or condolences, hopes for improved health.

'Don't pretend innocence,' he said furiously. 'Hypocrisy becomes no one. And you give yourself away.' He was shaking with anger now, and outrage.

She looked at his body bent over, as if hunched

into himself, protecting his most vulnerable parts, his heart, his abdomen, as if she were going to attack him physically. Was he so afraid of her, in his imagination, that he did it instinctively? She was no threat to him of any kind.

Clementine, she thought to herself. Or did she say it aloud?

'I will tell her,' he repeated. 'Don't think I won't.'

'Tell her what?' she said again.

'The wickedness you put in your poisonous letter, what else?' he snorted.

'I haven't written a letter that says anything at all about you to anyone. Why should I? Nobody I know has ever heard of you, let alone cares.'

'Don't play the fool with me,' he snapped. 'You wrote it, and I will tell Arthur about you. He will know you for what you are. Your threats are wasted. But I will not have Clementine hurt by your poisonous words. I forbid you to see her except at church, and in public, or I will tell everyone what a wicked, lying woman you are. Do you think they'll believe you about anything at all, once they know how you lied in court, before God himself? Think on that!'

'I haven't done anything.' Her voice was thick with tears of anger, of rage at the injustice of it, and yes, fear. The words came unbidden to her tongue. 'You say your wife ran away and sank to the gutter, then took her own life. God knows, you probably drove her to it.' The second she spoke she regretted it, but it was too late.

He took a step towards her, with both hands held out in front of him, as if he would take hold of her. Then he froze. 'You'd like that, wouldn't you? If I grasped you? You're trying to provoke me to strike you.'

'I don't know,' she said between her teeth. Her back was against the edge of the bench. She could go no further. 'I've never before known a man who would lash out at a woman. I suppose people are frightened or embarrassed and think no one would believe it, but—'

'And they won't believe you,' he interrupted, letting his hands fall. A half-smile came to his face. 'I should make sure that you look ridiculous, hysterical. I should say you were terrified that I would tell other people of your lies in court. You are a liar when you are faced with something you are afraid of.'

Should she deny it? He would know she was lying this time. What should she do? 'Then I had better tell the vicar myself,' she said desperately. 'Then there will be nothing left for you to do except gossip about a parishioner's confession. And no one would ever trust you again. That will be such unpleasantness for Clementine: her self-righteous husband a vicious gossip about other people's affairs.' And she walked past him, so close she actually brushed his arm, only avoiding touching it closer by leaning a little away. 'She might even decline the honour of marrying you.'

If he answered, she did not hear it. But then she was almost dizzy with relief at being out of his presence, and the mounting realisation of what she had done. She had committed herself to telling the vicar about the Exeter trial. Perhaps he already knew enough from their various conversations, but she thought not.

She walked down the path between the moss-encrusted gravestones, past the sombre yew trees towering darkly above the bare ground, then through the lich-gate and on to the road. In summer, the arch over it was covered with honeysuckle. Now, it was just the twisted vines tangled together, as if all life had drained from them and returned back into the earth.

She went straight across the road to the vicarage and knocked on the front door more loudly than she

51

had intended. She was afraid, and she probably looked it. Mrs Cross, the vicar's housekeeper, would be there at this time of day, probably making his lunch and preparing a dinner to be heated later.

Celia breathed in deeply and steadied herself.

The door opened and it was Arthur Roberson himself who stood in the hallway. He looked startled to see her. 'Celia! Come in. You seem distressed. Is something wrong?' He pulled the door wider and moved back to let her pass him.

He led her into the familiar, wood-panelled hall. It was only as the warmth enveloped her that she realised how cold she had become. Her mind raced as she tried to decide what she was going to say to him, how much she should tell him.

'Thank you,' she finally said, as she followed him into his study where the fire was burning with a fierce glow. 'I have to speak to you,' she said immediately. 'I'm sorry to come with no appointment, but this has just occurred and …' She realised she had no idea exactly what she intended to tell him, only that she meant to prevent Marlowe from telling the whole village his lurid view of the Exeter trial. Could she prevent that, if she encouraged Clementine to go through with her wedding, and never to confide anything concerning Marlowe, never to criticise him, support him in everything? Would that be enough?

'Celia,' the vicar said gently, 'what has happened? How can I help if I don't know?'

His mild face was filled with concern.

She sat down in the big armchair where so many other people had sat before, full of fear and hope ... and guilt.

At last, she knew the place to begin. 'Do you know anything more about the Exeter trial than what Seth Marlowe learned from the gutter press?' she asked.

'Yes,' he replied. 'I read *The Times*' account when it happened.'

This was painful. She cared what he thought of her more than she had expected. They shared a long history together, two lonely people trying to come to terms with it, and live up to their own beliefs of duty, not blind obedience, but kindness that was real. And with a focus on the end purpose, not the means of some grace or other. She had grown closer to Una as her strength had failed. She had watched her final losing struggle, and had done what she could to help ease her pain. Perhaps she should force herself to remember that Seth Marlowe had lost a sister, as well as his own wife in dreadful circumstances.

She began again. 'I did tell a lie from the witness stand.' She took a long, shaky breath. 'My lie was exposed. The innocent man did not suffer. I know what I did was wrong. The court knew the truth, so I received no punishment.' She stopped, uncertain what he would say. She had to silence Marlowe, for Hooper's sake as well as her own.

He answered with a frown of slow comprehension, 'If you have felt guilty for that, you shouldn't. You did what was right in your judgement and, it seems to me, in that of the judge. Your judgement was right and you have nothing to fear, or to apologise for. What is it that really troubles you?'

He had given her the perfect opening to tell him what Marlowe had threatened to do as a punishment if she did not leave Clementine strictly alone.

'Celia,' he said quietly, 'why is it that you came to tell me now? I cannot give you good counsel if I know only half the story, and perhaps the less important half.'

There was nothing to say but the truth. 'Seth Marlowe came to see me while I was arranging the flowers for the church. He said that if I continue my close friendship with Clementine, and in any way whatever speak against his wishes, he would tell

54

everyone that I had lied in the name of God and was guilty of perjury. And then no one would ever trust me again. You would be terribly disappointed in me. You might even ask me to leave the congregation …'

'I'm sorry. Poor Seth.' Roberson's face creased with pity. 'He has been so disappointed by the women he has loved that his views are warped. He can hardly believe that a lovely woman like Clementine could choose to marry him and be everything he wishes. I'm afraid you will have to give him time to realise his happiness, and trust in the goodness of God again. It is a lot to ask of you. I will speak to him and warn him against such a terrible piece of gossip.'

Celia bit her lip to stop herself from speaking too soon. He had not understood at all. How would she explain it to him? 'Clementine has no family,' she began again. 'Mr Marlowe does not want me to be a friend to her.' She heard her own voice become more urgent. 'He doesn't understand that she needs women friends, as well as a husband. Particularly now. She is going to embark on a new life. It is a big change for her. There are things she is a little nervous about, things that are new to her. I could …'

'He loves her very deeply,' the vicar said quietly.

'I know your husband only a little, but he seems a good man. Was he not gentle with you?'

Celia found herself blushing. The vicar had misunderstood her. That was not what she was referring to. 'Oh, you misunderstand! I mean simple things,' she said quickly 'Like cooking, laundry, learning to fit in with someone else's habits, and ways of doing things.'

'They will both need to change a little,' he said patiently. 'Perhaps it is better if we do not interfere. With the best will in the world, one might only make things worse. One is tempted to take sides, and it is really better if we do not. You would naturally understand Clementine almost completely, and Seth not at all. You cannot fault him for seeing it that way and being a little afraid.' He shook his head slowly. 'It is a very unexpected and newfound happiness for him, late in his life and when he thought there was no hope left. It is natural that he should fear losing it.' His lips tightened as the emotion overcame him. 'He has suffered terribly, you know. His first wife was a walking tragedy, and she did terrible damage to their only child. Perhaps it was not entirely her fault, but that did not lessen the grief for him.'

Celia did not answer. She realised how much she

liked Arthur Roberson, and how completely he did not understand what she was saying. He saw a different Seth Marlowe from the one she had seen. Was she wrong? Was she the one being judgemental, by failing to understand another person's pain … and misreading it?

'I know it is hard to forgive someone who has hurt a person we love, harder even than if they had hurt us,' he went on earnestly. 'But you must give him the chance to make Clementine happy, and I truly believe that she will fill with tenderness that awful wound in him. Is that not what you want for them both? There could be such blessings for him.' He smiled and his eyes softened. 'She is a beautiful woman, in her own way. She has a brightness about her, a light within. You will see a change in him. You will have to forgive the darkness and the pain in him, before it has been healed. We can most of us do it afterwards.'

She knew what he said was true, in principle, but he had not seen Marlowe's face, or the hand raised to strike her. Forgiveness was not supposed to be easy. She did not like Marlowe in the least bit, but was that not the point of it? Don't judge, especially when you don't know? Forgive anyway?

She reverted back to the issue that had brought her here. 'And the fact that I lied in court when I was under oath?'

'Was it easy to do?' he asked.

'No, I have never been more afraid.' Memory washed over her, as if the pain were raw and sharp. But it was the only thing that was right. 'I could not have lived with any alternative.' That was the truth. It had been the right thing to do at the time, and she felt it with an even deeper conviction now.

He smiled with great sweetness, even though she was still sure that he did not yet understand. He thought Marlowe a good man, and Clementine's love would gently unravel the hard knots in his soul. And was that true? Was it Celia who was unable to see the truth? Or far worse, unwilling to? What did he know of Marlowe that she did not – that was not her right to know? Or, for that matter, her wish. Did it matter, as long as he did not hurt Clementine?

Celia stood up, and the vicar stood also.

'I followed the Exeter case, at least some of it,' he said gravely, a shadow now across his face as memory of that tragedy returned. 'Don't let it twist your judgement, my dear. Hope, always keep hope.'

He walked towards the front door with her, and

just before he put his hand out to touch the handle, he spoke again. 'I shall have a word with Seth about gentleness. Clementine will need her women friends, especially if she should become with child. He must not think he can be everything to her. No one can do that. But it is natural enough, when you are in love, to imagine that you can. Clementine cares for you very much. I believe she lost her mother some time ago, and it is only natural. He can hold her far closer to him with a light hand than with a heavy one.'

Celia smiled back at him, forcing herself. She would have been so much happier if Clementine were marrying Arthur Roberson, but it would be unforgivable to say that. Clementine had never viewed him in that way, even if perhaps he had seemed to do so.

'Thank you, Vicar,' was all she answered.

Celia left the vicarage and started walking down the slight incline towards the cottage in which Clementine rented two rooms. It was barely sufficient for her needs, and left her little privacy, but she could afford it, as she cleaned the rest of the house for Miss Drew, the elderly woman who owned it. Clementine did a good deal of the cooking. That was a skill at which she excelled, possibly learned from her mother. But it was a very dependent situation, and one that she would be free of within a matter of months.

Or would she? If you were single, with only yourself and such skills as you possessed to depend on, life was difficult, but you could walk away from a situation if it became intolerable, even if all you could hope for was another domestic place similar to it, but with kinder conditions. Married, you were obliged to stay, whatever the circumstances. It might be happy, as Celia was. In fact, so happy at times she lay awake at night, almost afraid to go to sleep in case it all proved to be a dream and she would wake up alone, with only a memory.

She would lie listening to Hooper's even breathing in sleep, feeling the warmth of him beside her, thinking of his waking smile, his hand reaching out to touch her.

But what if Clementine married Marlowe? The way he had appeared to Celia, just hours ago: angry, vindictive, vengeful – how would he be with his young bride? The vicar had heard only Marlowe's side of the story. What would his wife's view have been? No one had heard Rose Marlowe's side, or that of the wayward daughter whose life was now on the street: Flavia had been her name. Marlowe spoke of her in hushed tones, as if she were dead, although he had no idea where she was. Literally dead or not, her soul was dead to him.

What did Clementine think of that? Surely her heart must ache for the girl, for Flavia Marlowe.

Now Celia was on her way to see Clementine, but to say what?

She dropped her pace from the swift walk it had been, produced by outrage, to a stroll. She walked down the road that ran between the neat cottages and the larger houses, many of them built of brick, and slate-roofed. Her anger was tempered by indecision, now that she weighed the choices. She had to see Clementine, if only to explain why she could no longer take the part of counsellor and friend that she had promised. It felt like something of a betrayal. She had promised, and promises should never be broken. But this was different. She pictured Seth Marlowe's face in her mind and had now no doubt whatever that he would carry out his threat if Celia disobeyed him.

What should she do? Tell Clementine as much of the truth as would make her understand, but no more? Not about the ugliness in his face, the hatred ... or was it fear? Was the vicar right, and Marlowe's first wife had hurt him so deeply that the wound was far from healed over? That, in fact, it was still bleeding?

Clementine was a natural healer. She had cared for many of the sick in the village, discreetly, but gratitude had not been silent. And she had nursed sick animals, sometimes with Celia's help. It was a great happiness they both treasured, watching over an injured cat or dog, feeding it regularly, seeing that it did not struggle to stand before its bones were healed, or pull out stitches before the skin mended over the torn flesh beneath. She smiled as she remembered one crazy white cat that had fallen out of a tree and broken so many bones they had thought it could not live. One old man had offered to kill it quickly, to save it from distress, but Clementine had fought him as if she were defending a child. Celia helped her nurse the cat, keeping it on a blanket before the stove in her kitchen. It had been wintertime, and bitterly cold, colder even than it was now. The cat healed, so there was nothing to show of the incident but a slight limp, and a disinclination to climb trees any more.

With their friendship and all the travails they had faced together, why should she not help Clementine with her wedding dress, with the arrangements, the guest list, with anything she wished with advice ... or silence? But always with happiness. Because Marlowe did not wish it? Was that going to be the pattern from now on? Marlowe wished it. Marlowe did not wish it. Could he not see that he was suffocating their friendship?

She crossed the road and passed a clump of bare trees that appeared like a lace tracing against the sky.

What could she say that was not merely mean spirited? What was practical? To stop any more poisonous letters, except she had no idea who had sent it. And Marlowe would almost certainly lash out at her if she tried. That would hurt two of the people she loved, Hooper and Clementine.

Surely the letter writer was someone who hated or feared Marlowe. Perhaps if she were more a part of the village, she could learn who it was? Sometimes the only defence was attack.

As she walked, she tried to think of all the people Marlowe had outraged or belittled at one time or another. There were lots of them, but were any hurt severely enough for this retaliation? It would take someone very brave, or very desperate, to fight back like this. Yet it had happened. Who might have secrets dark enough to provoke this? And, of course, sufficient knowledge of Marlowe's life to provide the weapon?

Would Arthur know? He would tell her he was bound to keep any secrets told to him. It was a sacred duty. But was it not also a sacred duty to prevent a crime? The wound to Clementine and to Marlowe himself would be deep – or it might be. What about the injury to the person who did such a thing? That would be lasting, a stain on the soul. Would Arthur not sooner prevent that?

It was, at the very least, a consideration.

But Arthur could only do that if he had some idea who it was. And did he?

She was at Clementine's door, surrounded by the bare vines of roses, and it was too late to turn back. Clementine was in the sitting room and had seen her through the window.

A moment later, Clementine opened the door. 'Miss Drew is asleep,' she said quietly. 'Come in.' She hesitated. 'You look concerned. Has something happened?'

Celia was still debating with herself what to say, or perhaps whether she should say anything at all, but Clementine's perceptiveness had robbed her of at least one choice: she could not deny it. She accepted the invitation and walked in quietly so as not to disturb the old lady.

Was it possible that Marlowe had already been here and said something?

Clementine led Celia into the sitting room, with its large, chintz-covered armchairs, flowered curtains, painted flower vases and photographs of people whose names Clementine admitted she had never known. She put another log on the fire, then sat down in the armchair with its back to the window and the fading afternoon light. 'What is it?' she asked. 'And don't tell me it's nothing. It's clear in your face, and however quick you are, it's going to be dusk by the time you go home and you'll be lucky if it is not raining.'

Celia plunged in, wishing now that she had not come. The last thing she wanted was to spoil Clementine's happiness, and yet how could she leave her sudden silence unexplained and her visit purposeless?

'I'm afraid I had something of a falling-out with Mr Marlowe,' she began. 'I think I was clumsy in what I said, and he has forbidden me to interfere in your arrangements. I didn't explain myself to his satisfaction. I'm very sorry. I wish you so much happiness, perhaps I was too concerned in my views …' She stumbled to a halt, knowing that she was not making the situation better.

Clementine met her eyes, then looked down at her hands that were folded in her lap. 'I'm sorry, too,' she said quietly. 'He has told me what happened. I can't help but feel he misunderstood you. I tried to tell him that, but I'm afraid I did not make a good job of it. He thought I was agreeing with you, saying I preferred your advice to his.' She looked up at Celia, her face pale and miserable.

Celia did not interrupt her. She could think of nothing to say.

'He sees me as disloyal. Celia, I can't do that to him. You understand, don't you? He has suffered so much. I have to earn his trust, after all that Rose did to him. He's so vulnerable.' Clementine looked very seriously at Celia. 'I can't imagine the pain he endured, and for years. He watched all the women he loved so dearly lose everything. His sister, Una, was ill most of her life, you know. Always delicate. Every winter they dreaded another chill, another fever, and each one left her weaker. Even though he had been expecting it, it broke his heart when she died. He and Arthur tried to console each other, but no amount of friendship in the world can combat the weight of grief, or the loneliness.'

Celia nodded silently. She knew exactly what Clementine meant. She, too, had put on a brave face, but sometimes the loneliness cut deep into her soul. This was Clementine's chance to give Seth Marlowe wisdom, care, and give love to someone who desperately needed it. Celia, of all people, should be happy for her. She despised herself for having any doubt about it, even for an instant. 'Of course,' she said quickly. 'Fears don't have to be sensible to hurt.'

Clementine smiled. 'Thank you. Of course, I want your advice, and your help. I'm suddenly aware of how little I know. It needs courage, doesn't it, to change, to share your life with someone else? But I know how happy you are, and how your mood changes your eyes, the way you smile, when you are going home and Mr Hooper is there, waiting for you. You climb the slope as if it were nothing. When you are in repose, you are smiling, as if your thoughts make you happy. I would like to be like that – like you.'

Celia could feel the heat rise up in her face. She had no idea she had been so easy to read. Had she come here without meaning? To waken a dream in Clementine's heart that, in the end, would only hurt her? She drew in breath to speak, then realised she had no idea what to say. But whatever it might have been, it was now not important. A mistake would matter terribly. 'I'm sure you will be the best that ever happened to him,' she said sincerely. It had never been about Seth Marlowe. She was beginning to have some pity for him, but the greater the distance between them, the more she liked it. 'I have no wish to intrude, or advise you against his wishes. Just to be here if you need me.'

Clementine blushed. 'I'm sure I will. But at least for now, I shall obey his wishes. I'm sorry. You could perhaps give me some domestic advice?'

'I doubt it,' Celia said with a rueful smile. 'You would do better to advise me. You are a better cook than I will ever be.'

'I learned from my mother.' Clementine stopped. 'I have told Seth a little about her, but …' she looked down, '… not a lot yet.'

'The right opportunity will arise,' Celia assured her, although she could not imagine how. But then, being in love, even a little bit, was something she could not imagine in Seth Marlowe. She was going to have to try a lot harder if she were to meet any of the standards of charity required of her.

'Thank you,' Clementine said, reaching out and clasping Celia's hand impulsively. 'If we are blessed with children, it will be a whole new life for Seth as well. I hope and believe in the future, and that love lasts.'

'Of course,' Celia agreed. There was nothing else she could do. The man Clementine saw was so utterly different from the one Celia had seen in front of the flowers in the church. But she understood that the thought of losing a marriage that promised to be brightest and best in Clementine's life, illuminating all the rest of it yet to come, was impossible to entertain. Celia, of all people, should understand. Her own life had changed in just the way Clementine's was about to. She could not be forgiven if she deliberately, or thoughtlessly, damaged that belief.

Celia stayed a few moments longer, then took her leave. It had become awkward to speak of other things, and artificiality was so unrelated to the friendship they had shared.

She walked very slowly, feeling more and more confused, as if she had sustained a loss, as if a piece of land with which she was familiar had broken off and was drifting away. It was only a break now, but she knew it would drift further away: the tide was set.

The wind was in her face and she bent a little to ease the chill of it. She thought of the small things she and Clementine had shared, their pleasure in the earliest flowers to bloom, the first leaves of the willow, like a chiffon scarf thrown over the bare branches. Or the dark moments, joining together to help someone in trouble, enjoying gentle humour that did not need words, only a glance and an under-standing, and the helpless laughter over something ludicrous. Would Seth Marlowe really stop all that?

Clementine would change. Would she honestly be happier? Or was her need for belonging at last, her hope for children, of a home and dignity of her own, respect where she believed that she had been toler-ated, and pitied – was it all worth that price?

Celia took a deep breath, and pushed down the cry rising from her chest. With surprise she realised her fists were clenched. It was not her choice to make. She must not even try.

Hooper was home early that evening. Celia was delighted to see him, and asked about his day, not only to avoid speaking of hers, but because she was genuinely interested. There was so much more life on the river than she had appreciated, simply looking at it from the shore. He had already told her about some of the great ships in the Pool of London: where they had come from, the vast seas they had sailed, the strange lands and wild shores. He described the tropics that he himself had seen in his years at sea, the blue and purple seas where the waters were broken by fish that flew! And in the north, the rivers of ice that barely moved, and the mountains of ice floating on the face of the sea.

Tonight, it was a little different. She had not realised it until he stopped speaking and leaned forward, his face grave, his voice still soft. 'What's wrong?' There was no doubt in his eyes. He would regard a denial as a lack of the trust that lay between them, unspoken but proved through both courage and grief. She was not prepared to lose that, for anything. 'Celia?'

'I was arranging flowers in the church this morning.' She sounded as if she were being evasive and she hated it. She must either tell him honestly, or not at all. She could not bear the thought of a lie between them, like a rock in the centre of the bed.

'Seth Marlowe came in.' She waited for him to interrupt, and he did not. 'He told me not to give Clementine any advice, of any sort, but particularly in personal matters. He said he would give her all the counsel she needed. She was to be his wife, and that changed everything.'

Hooper's face darkened, but he did not interrupt.

She could see in the line of his mouth that he was preparing for something he would not like, maybe would not even tolerate. 'I argued with him, told him that she would need a woman to share certain concerns with. I shouldn't have had to detail that, and he wasn't listening anyway. Effectively, he wants me out of her circle. Polite in church, but nothing more than that. I know she will obey him; she is determined to love him, to protect him.' She heard her own voice; it sounded as if she were looking for words to cover a lie. It wasn't a lie, except by omission. That was just as dishonest. No, more so, because she was lying to herself as well.

He was waiting. Did she have to tell him about the threat? She would very much rather not. But if Marlowe thought she had defied him, he would fulfil his threat. And Hooper would know that she had lied. Even if he didn't work it out, Marlowe would make sure he learned. She swallowed. 'He threatened me.'

Hooper stiffened. 'What?'

Now she wanted to get it over. 'He knows about the Exeter trial. He knows that I lied under oath. That's perjury.'

'You told the truth in the end. And you will not be charged,' he said levelly, but his voice shook, and it was out of anger, not fear.

'I know,' she agreed. 'But would anyone else see it like that? Would Clementine, if he told her that I would lie, even with my hand on the Bible, swearing to God that it was the truth?' She needed his answer, and she needed him to be completely honest. 'Would you, if you didn't love me?'

He put his hand over hers gently. 'I'm glad you know I do. Are you afraid?'

'Yes. No. No …' She stumbled over the words. Not deeply afraid, not yet, anyway. 'But I care about Clementine. I know a lot of what she feels.' She smiled very slightly. 'It was me, just a few years ago. She wants to marry and have children, and she knows her past has cost her all her chances so far.' She looked at him earnestly. 'She's terribly vulnerable, John. And I know what that feels like. It's so easy to protect ourselves by not hoping, not letting us care enough to be hurt. And people see it. She would pay any price herself, as long as no one else suffers. She truly believes she could love Marlowe enough, make him feel safe, and quell the fear inside him so that he'll be happy, and change. I've seen it happen to others.'

'Most of us can be happy when we have what we want,' he pointed out. 'The true victory lies in being kind, even when we don't have it.'

'I know,' she admitted. 'But isn't any victory worth having? And who are we to judge anyway?' She meant that as plainly as she said it, and watched his face to see the understanding in it, and possibly the annoyance.

He smiled wryly. 'No one,' he admitted. 'You have the perfect reason to give him all the latitude Clementine asks. This time. What about next time?'

'Next time?' For a moment, she was confused.

'Next time he asks you to do something, or not to do it, and threatens to tell people about your part in the Exeter case, and my part in the mutiny on the *Mary Grace* … if you don't do as he wishes, or take his advice regarding Clementine, or Arthur Roberson, or anyone else.'

She froze. Realisation of all that he had said, and in so few words, crept over her like ice water. She was surprised she could still breathe.

'I'm sorry,' he whispered. 'Do you want less than the truth?'

She had no answer. Or to be more exact, she had several, and none of them was what she wanted to believe, or even to acknowledge.

He waited again.

'Don't you think he'll change, after he marries Clementine?' she asked, searching his face. 'When he's happy, or beginning to taste real safety of the heart?'

'Oh, my dear.' He shook his head. 'Would you really base your judgement on the probability of a change of heart? Do you think that will make Clementine happy? She holds him to decency, refraining from blackmail, only by pleasing him?'

'I didn't say ...' she began, then stopped. 'Do you think he'd really do it? I mean, tell everyone about the Exeter trial? Wasn't it just an empty threat to frighten me?'

'And does it? Frighten you?' he questioned.

'No. I mean ...' She thought of how much it hurt if people thought ill of her. This was her home.

She had nowhere else where she belonged. There would be no defence against it, because the whispers would never be specific. People were embarrassed to repeat gossip, said they didn't believe it, and yet they did. 'What's wrong with him?' she demanded suddenly. The stories were old, and as hard to catch as a shadow, before anyone corrected it. But the suspicion, the doubt, all remained after the fact had disappeared or had been forgotten.

'Celia.'

'Yes.'

'Is that really what Clementine wants? When she is alone, and vulnerable, possibly with child for the first time? She will need you for all sorts of things, but most of all for advice without criticism; friendship, someone to walk with her along a path she doesn't know. When you're feeling strange and vulnerable, what you need more than anything else is kindness.'

She said nothing. Suddenly, ridiculously, there were tears in her eyes. This was stupid. But he was right, that was the key to it: kindness. She loved Hooper profoundly, and what mattered even more sometimes, she was sure he loved her. But she still had moments of strangeness, times when she needed to be alone, not to have to account to anyone. Least of all someone who was always going to be there, seeing, noticing even silly mistakes. And there were bound to be mistakes. Everyone made them. The gift of love, to overlook, even forget, was one of the most important anyone could have.

Which brought her back to everything Arthur Roberson had said. Wasn't that the real gift of Christmas, which they were fast approaching?

She lifted her head a little. 'He only threatened,' she said quite clearly. 'He didn't do anything. I don't think he will.' She thought of the other things Marlowe had spoken of, the letter: should she tell Hooper of it?

'Because of Clementine?' he asked, and there was no belief in his voice. 'Is it for her sake that you want to spare him?'

She was caught. She felt a tightness of reason closing around her, preventing her movement. 'I don't want to be the sort of person he is. He's always finding fault, seeing guilt where there's only ignorance or ordinary mistakes. Most people don't really commit sin, John. They have their eyes on their own needs, and are unintentionally robbing other people. It is self-preservation, not wickedness. Thoughtlessness, if you like.'

'But is it just selfishness?' he probed. 'Me first and second, you third, maybe.'

She did not answer. How could anything be so cloudy, and yet so strong? She hated lying to Hooper. And such gaping omissions were lies. Powerful lies, lots of them, could be built by omitting one terrible fact. It was the cornerstone of a wall that would eventually close him out. One lie created the necessity of another, and another.

Hooper was a policeman. Sometimes she forgot that. She thought of him on the river, especially when the weather was harsh. Often, he came home cold and exhausted, and she learned to deduce from his silences, the gentleness of his touch and his need to be with her, that he had seen tragedy. But he never described it to her. The funny things he told her about, even the tales of the men he worked with, their names, their successes and sometimes their failures – she felt as if she knew them through his eyes. It all painted a picture of his life that engaged her, and had led her to understand him so much better.

She wished she had something of equal interest

to share with him, but everything about her life was so small by comparison, so domestic and repetitive. She had made herself feel very dull, until he had pointed out how many times she had helped someone, and had learned to understand them. People turned to her, because she made time to listen to them.

'All I do is listen,' she had said sadly. 'So often, I can't help.'

'Listening does help,' he had answered. 'Most of the despair I've seen is because there was no one to listen.'

Perhaps that was true. It was a sweet thought.

'Well?' he pressed, bringing her unwillingly back to the present.

'He accused me of having written a very horrible letter to him,' she answered. 'About the death of his first wife. Apparently anonymous, and accusing him of awful things. He didn't actually quote anything. I think he couldn't bring himself to repeat the accusations. But if I didn't stop, he said, he would tell Clementine.'

'He won't,' Hooper said with certainty. 'He doesn't want you to know what's in it exactly, and certainly doesn't want Clementine to know.'

She met his eyes very directly. 'John, he thinks I wrote it. So, I must know what's in it,' she protested.

He ignored her words. 'Does he want other people to know what's in it? Did he give any clue to what it's about?'

'Something to do with Rose, his first wife. She died tragically.'

'Did you know her?'

'No, that was before he came to live here.'

Hooper sat silent for a few minutes.

Now it was she who waited.

He stood up slowly. She started to rise, but he held out his hand in a sign to stop her. 'No, I'm going to do this alone. You stay here, and lock the door behind me.'

'He's not going to …' she began. Then she remembered his upraised hand in the church room with the flowers.

He caught her hesitation. 'What?' he demanded.

She said nothing, trying to decide how much to tell him.

'Celia?'

She looked up. His face was very grave, his eyes unblinking.

She would break something between them if she did not tell the truth. He would afterwards never be sure she was being totally honest. That was something Marlowe was not going to take from her. 'He made as if to strike me, in the church flower room ... but he didn't.'

Hooper did not ask why she had not told him before. Perhaps he understood. 'Keep the door locked after dark. You did before I came here, you must still do it.' The ghost of a smile lit his face for a minute, a softness. 'For my sake. I want to think you're safe beside the fire.'

She nearly argued, then she realised the intense seriousness in his eyes and sat back immediately. 'Yes, John,' she said with an obedience that held an echo of humour in it, but also one of the safest, most precious things she felt.

Hooper sat and watched Arthur Roberson. Seen in the now dramatic glow of the gas lamps in the vicarage sitting room, Roberson's face was startlingly stronger than in the western light outside, and more deeply marked by its lines. It was a more interesting face than Hooper had supposed. How many other people's griefs had this man listened to and without ever sharing his own? Who did he go to when doubts or profound loneliness assailed him?

'Perhaps apology is necessary for forgiveness,' Hooper suggested. 'I don't know. But it is necessary for Celia. She is concerned for Clementine.'

'Clementine may be the salvation of Seth Marlowe,' Roberson said with a slow, sad smile. 'She is a gentle creature, but not by any means weak.'

'That does not mean she cannot be hurt,' Hooper pointed out.

'Life is not avoiding pain, Mr Hooper. It is learning how to deal with it with grace and courage. The lives of great people are stories of victory over pain and loss, major ills, or the long, quiet putting-up graciously with difficulty, and thinking of others.'

There was nothing Roberson had said that Hooper could disagree with. In fact, within him, its truth touched chords of admiration at the silent victories of great lives. But it had nothing to do with Seth Marlowe threatening Celia.

Hooper smiled apologetically. 'And not passing on your pain to other people, using it as an excuse for lashing out. Isn't that part of your task, to help us achieve that?' Hooper was silent for several moments, but nothing came to his mind to help the vicar. His emotions were occupied with the distress he had read in Celia's face, heard in her voice. She identified with Clementine in her loneliness, in her apprehension at making mistakes as she set out on a new course in her life, with no mother or sister or aunt to guide her.

He remembered with tenderness his own early months with her after they were married. She had tried so hard to hide her nervousness. Suddenly, she was burning dishes she had cooked beautifully a hundred times. She was meticulous in laundering everything in sight. He had teased her, and sometimes he had made mistakes, taken something too lightly and hurt her, when he was trying to pass over it. He almost acknowledged his error, then realised the only tactful thing was not to mention it. A gentle turn was sufficient, casually, a quick word of acknowledgement of a kindness, something said or done to please him.

And that worked in the other direction as well. He, too, had been serious. In particular, he had been physically awkward, afraid of hurting or embarrassing her. It was she who had moved gently and assured him. He blushed even now at the thought of it.

He must protect Clementine, because in a way she stood in Celia's place. Did he even imagine that Marlowe loved Clementine as he loved Celia? And had he any right at all to judge?

Roberson was watching him, waiting.

'When you are embarking on something new,' Hooper said, 'something that has to succeed for your happiness, it takes high courage, or else very little imagination, not to fear mistakes that will cost you much.' There was not enough room for mistakes, and no one else to turn to for advice, for comfort, for encouragement to mend the breach, whatever it was. 'We must try to encourage Marlowe not to forbid Clementine from having friends,' Hooper continued. 'She is young, she needs friends with whom she has something in common. A little laughter, light-heartedness. She's not …' He stopped, seeing Roberson trying to find words.

'He will change,' Roberson said earnestly. 'Misery, loneliness, can alter people. He has suffered more or less alone for—'

'His wife left him,' Hooper said, aware that it was harsh.

'A tragedy,' Roberson said quickly. 'She was …'

'Deeply unhappy,' Hooper said for him. 'Do you know why?'

'Not really,' Roberson said immediately. 'Seth didn't live here then. He told me something of the pain he felt. In confidence, of course. She was a woman with …' He shook his head. 'I can't discuss it, Mr Hooper. I'm sure you have seen many tragedies that you were not free to speak of to others. I sometimes wonder how you keep your balance. Are you free to discuss those with your wife?'

Hooper thought he had been about to use her given name. Perhaps he even thought how he would like to have had someone gentle, and far wiser and more observant than others supposed. He smiled. 'She doesn't ask, but yes, sometimes late in the evening, when I can't let go of it and go to bed, I'll tell her bits and pieces.'

'It helps.'

'Yes, it helps,' Hooper agreed.

Roberson smiled, and it was a startlingly sweet expression. 'You are a very fortunate man, Mr Hooper. Don't rob Seth Marlowe of a chance to find his better self, and give Clementine the opportunity to give it to him. And to find her best self, too. She is a healer, you know. I don't mean with medicine, I mean with kindness, patience, generosity to forgive, and laughter. She can share his way of life with him. He could be reborn, as it were. Forgiveness is a miracle, Mr Hooper, in more ways than perhaps you know.'

Hooper drew in a slow breath. 'Yes, I do know that very well. I have been forgiven for more than anyone can deserve. I've made mistakes, some of them big ones, that have affected other people. But only a few earn self-forgiveness without reparation. And true regret means sorrow, not excuses or justification.'

'I know,' Roberson agreed quietly. 'Clementine will help, and Celia, perhaps, in time.' He leaned forward. 'Give them a chance, Mr Hooper, please?'

There was only one possible answer. 'Of course, Vicar. But not at Celia's expense. Please convince Mr Marlowe that if he gossips about her, in any way, I will hear of it, and I will not forgive.'

Roberson drew in his breath, and then was silent.

'It's your calling to defend the innocent, Vicar, as well as the repentant.'

'I know that, Mr Hooper. As yours is, I believe. You catch the guilty, but far better if you can prevent the crime in the first place.'

'Yes,' Hooper admitted with a smile at the vicar's gentle but powerful argument. 'I think you would like to prevent Seth Marlowe from spreading vicious rumours about people, rather than, for instance, trying to mend the damage after it is done. Deep damage. Poison cannot be sucked out the same as it can be taken in. I think you know that.'

'I disagree—' Roberson began, but Hooper would not let him finish.

'Take a casual piece of slander,' Hooper went on. 'About a man, for example. His wife believes it, because she thought the person who gave it to her was honourable. Everyone knew she believed it. So, when it divided the family, sons and daughters against each other, other people took sides. Then it was proved false. Everyone apologised to him, but can he ever forget that they had believed it? Above all, that his wife had believed it of him? You can't mend that. Apologise, repent all you like, the wound is there.'

'I suppose you are right,' Roberson conceded. 'Then we had better not believe it all of Seth either.

Give him the chance to make Clementine happy. Think well of him, and he may live up to it.'

'And my wife?' Hooper asked. 'Will you ask him, even tell him, that he must not accuse her of having written anyone a poisonous letter?' He saw the horror in the vicar's face and stopped.

'Poisonous? How very dreadful.' Roberson's voice was hoarse with shock, and his skin was pale. 'He must … he must have been shaken to the core.' He was clearly searching for a reason to forgive. 'Did he tell you what it said?' He put his hand up to rub his brow, as if it might somehow get rid of the horror of what he had heard. He looked up at Hooper. 'He was confused, at a loss …' he attempted to explain Marlowe's actions.

'In a temper,' Hooper replied.

Roberson shrugged, regret in his face. 'Perhaps.'

'Most people would not believe it,' Hooper said, hoping that was true, but he knew how cruel whispers could be. He thought of what Celia had said to him. 'And, of course, it is a dreadful stain on the soul of whoever writes such things. Are they not also important?'

Roberson held up one hand. 'I know, I know. I will speak to Marlowe. And … and I will think hard as to who it may be who would have written such a thing. I admit, I have no idea ...'

'Thank you,' Hooper acknowledged.

At home, he had to explain it to Celia. He did not want to disillusion her about the vicar's willingness, or even his ability, to confront Seth Marlowe and tell him some of the bitter truths about his own behaviour, his criticism and his judgement.

'He'll try,' he said gently to Celia.

They were standing in the kitchen, Celia at the bench while she boiled the kettle to make tea and put out his favourite biscuits. She turned round to face him. 'You mean he will not succeed? Seth Marlowe will listen politely to Arthur, but then continue exactly the same way as before. He knows all the arguments and has all the right quotations, almost entirely from the Old Testament. He can find a verse of damnation to cover any situation.'

'I'm not arguing with you, love,' Hooper said quietly, putting his hand out to touch her. 'That's why we can't let it go. Marlowe will use that charge again, when he needs it, or feels it will serve him. Or simply loses his temper.'

She bit her lip and nodded slowly.

Hooper had no certainty what was on her mind, but he thought it might be Exeter, and Celia's cousin's death. There were realities one had to face. 'Forgiveness is his job,' he said, referring to Roberson.

'I know,' she said quietly, and there was deep, aching pain in her eyes as she stared at him. 'It sounds good, but it can become an excuse for always turning the other cheek, or if you want to be more honest, looking the other way.'

He was taken aback by her candour. She had known Arthur Roberson for years, listened to him with respect, and quite often, but she was not unaware that at least some of his gentleness was an evasion of unpleasantness. It was easy to do and, at least at first, it did not offend the conscience. Especially if you did not look any further ahead than what was best for the person with you. It was so easy to want to say what they needed to hear, at that moment. How did you think ahead to the next day, or week, never mind the time when you needed to deal with the next slip, the result, the time when you were proved wrong?

'Repentance?' he probed, then immediately wished he had not, but it was too late. He saw the confusion in her face.

'I'm not sure,' she admitted. 'I used to think it was beautiful to forgive unconditionally. And it has to be unconditional or it is not real. Beautiful for the healing of the one forgiven, and perhaps even more for the one who forgives, asking nothing. But now I'm not sure. Is it only because I am involved? I can forgive as long as I am not threatened? That's pretty poor, isn't it? In fact, it's first-class hypocrisy. It's just ...' She looked close to tears. 'It's so easy to make it sound right, and I don't know what the answer really is.'

She was asking Hooper obliquely at least to suggest the answer. And he could not. It was not the time to guess. Instead, he closed his hand over hers, and slowly her fingers tightened around his.

When Hooper was gone, Roberson remained sitting in the big chair beside the fire, turning over in his mind what he had heard. It saddened him and he concentrated on that feeling, because the one that lay just a little behind it was so much worse. He admitted to himself now: it was fear for Clementine. He had no doubt that her optimism, her laughter and gentleness would ease the pain that held Marlowe's heart so tightly. How long would it take him to learn to trust her? And how would she bear it if he took too long? If he doubted her, and she had to stand alone against his distrust?

Roberson would not willingly allow anyone to hurt Clementine, but would he know? She would not confide in him if anyone did, of that he was certain. He put the guard up against the fire and went out into the hall.

He put on his warmest coat, hat and scarf, pulled the gloves out of the pocket and set out to see Seth Marlowe, battling his way against the wind, which had shifted to the east and become colder. He had gone over and over it in his mind, trying to find the best way to word what he had to say. There was a lot to know about Seth that he had not told Celia Hooper. In fact, over twenty-five years in this community, since he had first come here as a curate at the beginning of his career, he had learned far more secrets, hopes and fears, false guilt and real, than he wanted to recall. That, and his own doubts, were the heaviest burdens he knew.

It had been much easier in the beginning, when he and Una were first married. She had shared so much. It made his heart ache to recall how sweet she had been. Then she had become ill. It had seemed slow at the time, a cold that had stayed longer than earlier ones. Then she grew tired much more easily. There were fevers and chills, weariness, then at last the knowledge that she was not going to get better. He had struggled to accept that. What was the use in believing in a God of miracles if He would not, or could not cure Una?

Had he tried hard enough, prayed humbly enough? At dark moments, he believed that if he had been better, stronger in his faith, Una would have lived. What would he give to have that guilt lifted? All he could do was plead for forgiveness for others, and make it wide enough and deep enough to include himself as well.

He reached Seth Marlowe's door and knocked. It was opened almost immediately and Seth stood in the handsome hallway. He saw the vicar and his grave expression relaxed.

'Come in, Arthur, come in.' He stepped back invitingly.

Roberson followed him through the austere hall and into the well-furnished, very masculine sitting room with its brown leather upholstered chairs and dark Turkish carpet. There were very few pictures on the mantel, and none of them was personal. There was a polished wooden desk against one wall. The bookshelves were packed, even a few books spilled over on to a polished mahogany table. It was the refuge of a very serious man. He could not imagine Clementine comfortable in here. But then, perhaps, he did not know her as well as he imagined. It was a feeling he must discipline. Clementine was going to marry Marlowe. It was, in fact, already decided.

He sat down where Marlowe indicated, then Marlowe himself sat down, comfortably, one leg crossed over the other. This was a place where he was very obviously relaxed, effortlessly in control, and comfortable. A large fire burned in the grate beneath the fine classical Adam fireplace.

'What may I do for you, Arthur?' he asked. 'Plainly, something is on your mind.'

Roberson hated confrontation. He saw his role as peacemaker, not warrior. But there was no evading this, for Clementine's sake.

'Seth, it has come to my attention that you have been the victim of a very unpleasant letter. Anonymous, of course. People who write such things never have the courage to sign their names.' He stopped, seeing the anger harden in the other man's eyes, and his face set in well-worn lines of displeasure.

'It is not your concern, Arthur,' Marlowe said, his voice altered in tone, and edged with real temper. 'I did not wish to trouble you with it, and I still do not.'

'I am afraid it is no longer your choice,' Roberson replied.

'Indeed, it is,' Marlowe retorted.

'Not now that you've chosen to accuse Celia Hooper of having written it.'

Marlowe's eyebrows rose. 'Do you know that she didn't?' Marlowe challenged. 'Why did she mention it at all? Does she expect you to fight to clear her name? I assure you, that is not necessary. I have told no one else. But if she does it to other people, they may not be so forbearing.'

'We will deal with others, if they exist.' Roberson sat perfectly still, but he was uncomfortable, his body rigid in the well-padded armchair. Now that he had begun, he felt his own anger at Marlowe for this attack on Celia. 'You accused Celia, and she naturally told her husband, since any attack on her reputation must automatically affect him.'

'She lied, you know? Under oath. Apart from the offence against God, it is perjury under the law.' Marlowe's eyes were hot and angry.

For a moment, Roberson was going to answer that

it was none of Seth Marlowe's business. Then the wiser, cleverer choice came to his mind. 'Yes, I do know,' he answered. 'The law did not find fault with her. It seems that you do. In spite of her repentance, and apology, you accuse her, find her guilty without a hearing, and condemn her. What happened to the repentance and forgiveness you agreed with so intensely only last Sunday?'

Marlowe's face flushed hot red. 'She is an opinionated woman, a rebel against the laws of God, a troublemaker. I will not have her poisoning Clementine's mind with her ideas.'

'What ideas, Seth?' Roberson asked softly, but he could feel the emotion stirring in him: anger and distress. 'Do you really believe she wrote that letter to you?'

'It was a woman's hand!'

'And it was posted locally?'

'It was delivered by hand. It was in my letterbox, here in my home, so whoever penned it knows my address. And it was written by someone who knows me well enough to be aware of what lies to invent that would hurt the most. And would poison Clementine against me. They were terrible things.' Now the colour had drained from his face and he was shaking. Even the hands knotted in his lap were white-knuckled.

Roberson felt a wave of pity engulf him. Seth had already suffered the loss of his first wife, whose death was by her own deliberate act. The sins of his daughter were, in his mind, a disgrace worse than death. Now, at last, a bright future, happiness with a young and truly beautiful woman, perhaps even children, were almost within his reach. No wonder a terrible fear gripped him.

But Celia Hooper was not at fault. Roberson believed her absolutely. And she, too, had had to wait a long time for happiness. He also knew that John Hooper would not stand by and see her slandered without lifting a hand to help her. If Marlowe attacked Celia, he would pay a very heavy price for it.

Marlowe was waiting, his anger and his fear seeming to grow.

'Seth, you do not know it was Celia,' Roberson began again, this time more urgently. 'You only believe it because you fear her influence on Clementine. If you accuse her, however obliquely, you will lay the whole matter wide open. The contents of the letter, whatever they are, would become public. Is that what you want?'

Marlowe gripped the arms of the chair. 'She won't dare do that. They would force her to bring the charge, and her husband would lose his job in the River Police. Then how would they keep him from being tried and hanged for his part in the mutiny on the *Mary Grace*?' He sat more stiffly upright. 'And even if they didn't hang him, they would lose the roof over their heads, and everything else as well.' He smiled very slightly. 'And how would her reputation fare then?'

'Better than yours, Seth,' Roberson replied tartly. 'And Clementine might be loyal to you in this, but you will have hurt her deeply. Is that what you want to do?'

Marlowe hesitated. 'Celia Hooper is not a suitable influence on Clementine. You can't argue with that.'

'Perhaps Clementine would be a good influence upon Celia,' Roberson suggested.

'Clementine is young, alone, and she is vulnerable. I must protect her from that.'

Was that true? Roberson thought of all he knew about Clementine. Pictures came to him from the past: Clementine with her face lifted to the sun, smiling at the warmth and light. Clementine finding the first primrose in spring, or laughing at lambs playing in the field, only a few days old and yet already sure footed. Clementine with her arms around a crying child, whispering to him, or laughing heartily at a risqué joke, and then at Roberson because he was slow to admit he also thought it was really funny. And if Seth were so persuasive that he would not let her have women friends, he certainly would not let her keep her friendship with Roberson, and that hurt even more than he expected.

No, he was being less than honest, because the truth had a unique pain. Once she was married to Seth Marlowe, he would own all those moments that were so sharp in memory, so sweet. But that's all they would be, memory, growing old like a carefully pressed flower between the pages of a book, beautiful, but not alive any more. Odd how, if you did it properly, pressed flowers, even years old, kept their colour.

The truth of it was that he loved Clementine. He had thought himself too old for her, too staid, and he did not want to lose the friendship they had by asking for something, anything more. But he was the same age as Seth, and Seth had asked her, and she had accepted. If Roberson really loved her, then he would want her happiness, even if it was with Marlowe.

Marlowe had been talking for some time and Roberson had not been listening. That happened rather often. He admitted it, he found Seth a bore.

'I'm sure she will earn the respect of the other women in the church,' Marlowe was saying.

'That sounds like a cold thing,' Roberson said with unusual honesty.

Marlowe's eyebrows shot up. 'I beg your pardon?'

Roberson was about to phrase the whole thought more charitably, then changed his mind and said quite clearly what he thought. 'Clementine is young, Seth, barely over thirty. The respect of tightly corseted middle-aged church women is hardly the stuff of happiness. They don't like the same things, they aren't interested in the same things, and they don't laugh at the same things. In fact, as far as I can see, most of them don't laugh at all.'

'Church is not the place for loud laughter and light mindedness, Arthur. You know that as well as I do!' Marlowe answered. 'The last thing you want is someone giggling in the church. It is an affront to God.'

Roberson quite unaccountably lost his temper. 'Don't be so damnably stupid, Seth! The laughter of children is music to God.'

'We are not children!'

'Yes, we are. Underneath the sombre clothes, which we wear both as armour against intrusion, and to hide the fact that we are actually all the same, and all different, and both noble and absurd, we are always vulnerable,' Roberson stated with absolute assurance.

Marlowe rose to his feet. 'You are tired, Arthur, and a little distraught. This whole matter has upset you. I should do you the favour of forgetting this unfortunate conversation.'

Roberson stood up, too. 'I don't doubt that you will, not for my comfort of mind, but for your own.' He knew the next words were cruel, partly because they were true. 'But you would be wiser to remember them. Clementine is young and she is very well liked, not only by women who perhaps have forgotten how to laugh, maybe because life has disappointed them, but by the elderly who don't care any more what other people think, only what truly matters to them, and may not have much longer to enjoy it and give thanks. And by the young, who see the joy and the absurdity in new life, and hope for everything.'

'Have you been drinking?' Marlowe asked, his eyes narrowed. Then he had a sudden flash of inspiration. 'You care for her yourself!' he said. It was almost a challenge.

Roberson felt the heat flush up his face, to the degree that it was useless to deny it.

Marlowe looked very directly into the vicar's eyes. 'Then I had better warn you: she has accepted my offer of marriage, and you are standing at the very gates of sin if you entertain any thoughts of influencing her against me for your own ends … however you may disguise that to yourself as being in her interest.' And with that he strode to the door and flung it open for Roberson to leave.

The next day, having only light duties, Hooper set out to learn what he could of Seth Marlowe's past, in those years before he came to live in the same parish as Celia. It was simple enough to find this in parish records. Hooper was surprised to learn that it was no more than four years ago – or, to be precise, three years and ten months.

When he went across the river to the parish in

question, and the Church of St Stephen, it took a while to locate the vicar, the Reverend Mr Soames, who had no hesitation recalling Seth Marlowe.

The man was writing his sermon for the following Sunday and seemed delighted to have any excuse whatsoever for putting it aside. He was a big man with a handsome, almost white moustache, who wore his black cassock with the aplomb of a dowager in her best gown, and invited Hooper to come in and sit down by the fireside.

'What can I do for you, Mr … Hooper … is it?' Soames asked, coming across the floor of the spacious vicarage sitting room with a fire blazing in the hearth. Christmas ornaments, coloured paper chains and red wax candles were much in evidence. He saw Hooper's glance. 'Ah, yes! For the grandchildren, you know. Besides, my wife likes it. Bit of a change from the regular round of cleaning up after one and thinking what to cook for dinner.' He smiled in an avuncular fashion. 'What is it you would like to know about Mr Marlowe? He was here for some two or three years. I hope he is not unwell?'

'I think he is in excellent health,' Hooper replied, watching the reaction in Soames's face, which as yet he could not read. It seemed kind, filled with good humour, and yet his hand on his lap was tight, fingers gripping at nothing but cloth.

'Then what may I help you with?' Soames did not appear any more at ease, but his smile widened a little. 'Who did you say you are, again? Mr Hooper of …?'

'I belong to the parish in which Mr Marlowe now lives,' Hooper replied. He did not yet wish to mention the Thames River Police. As far as he knew, there was nothing that would have concerned them. Anonymous threatening letters were not in their purview.

'And your concern about Mr Marlowe?' Soames was a trifle more aggressive now, although the expansive smile did not change.

'He is being harassed by a rather unpleasant letter – anonymous, of course. Such things usually are. It is not very serious, but it is unpleasant.'

'Did Seth ask you to pursue this for him?' Soames was now openly incredulous. He shifted in his seat a little to face Hooper more directly.

'No.' Hooper had planned to be honest in everything he could. 'But he has accused my wife of being involved – in fact, of actually writing it.' Anger slurred Hooper's voice, although he had not intended it to.

'Oh dear.' Now Soames was taken completely off guard. That was something very clearly he had not expected. 'I'm so sorry.' He drew his breath in, made a decision, and let it out again. 'Naturally, your wife is innocent, and distressed by it. I'm so sorry. You wish to know if it could be anyone from Marlowe's past, here at St Stephen's?'

'Yes,' Hooper agreed. 'We need to put a stop to it. The longer it goes on, the more innocent people are going to be hurt. Which I suppose is the purpose of such letters. They stir up suspicions in everyone.'

'Quite so.' Soames was clearly perceptive of the dangers, and yet Hooper had the distinct feeling that he was not entirely displeased. 'And what makes you think that it might be someone from St Stephen's, rather than a present acquaintance that he has … upset?'

'He upsets people?' Hooper asked as innocently as he could.

'I'm afraid he was inclined to be a trifle …' Soames searched for the word, and then said, '… judgemental. And he was not always as discreet as he might have been with his opinions. I imagine a few people would have been delighted to catch him out in something.' He started to smile, and then rapidly changed his mind.

Hooper affected not to have noticed. 'In what might anyone have caught him out?' He smiled, only mildly curious.

'Unfortunately, I don't know.' Soames shrugged his heavy shoulders. 'Most unchristian of me, but I would dearly have liked to …'

This time Hooper did smile. 'I like an honest man,' he said sincerely. 'Any ideas?'

Soames gave a weighty sigh and let it out slowly. 'If his wife was as great a failure as he says, one can only feel sorry for him. He must have been a saint to have put up with her.'

'What were her failings?' Hooper disliked asking this. He had never met the poor woman, but felt a certain pity for her. It was easy to brand someone as a failure, and look no further. When they believed it of themselves, it sooner or later became true.

Soames sighed. 'Everything. She was wayward, disobedient, immodest; she laughed too loudly, and at the wrong things; she dressed badly; she was argumentative, she even lied, particularly to him. Above all, she was a bad mother. I hate to repeat that, but that was how Seth Marlowe saw her, and I presume that is what you want to know.'

'Did other people see her that way?'

'You may ask my wife, if you wish. She didn't know Rose Marlowe because she died before her husband came here. But I believe she knew one or two people who did know her.'

'Very generous of you,' Hooper accepted. 'We've got to put a stop to these letters. They can do so much damage. And Marlowe is engaged to be married again. To a friend of my wife, a very nice young woman.'

Soames looked startled. 'Really? I wonder if the writer of the letter could be a previous admirer of his. How young is she? Marlowe must be over fifty by now, for heaven's sake.'

Hooper had a sudden vision of Arthur Roberson's gentle face puckered with sorrow, and then something deeper. Anger? Jealousy? No, it was regret. He pulled his thoughts back to the present. 'I'm not sure of her age, and I don't believe she knew him before he arrived in our village. I should ask my own wife; she has known Clementine far longer than I have. I ...' He had been going to mention Roberson, then he changed his mind. This man might well know him. 'Thank you,' he said.

Mrs Soames proved to be a quiet woman, even homely, but with a quick wit and a kind eye. Her hair was exceptionally beautiful – thick, light brown, and falling in soft waves that completely escaped the rather random pins she had put in it to hold it up.

'So, Seth Marlowe is going to marry again?' she said with alarm.

Hooper tried to keep his face expressionless, and was not at all sure he succeeded. 'Yes, and his friends are hoping it will bring him some happiness, and ease from the grief that seems to be always just over his shoulder.'

'How well you put it, Mr Hooper,' she responded with enthusiasm. 'Not like a ghost that haunts him, as many people have said, but like a cloak he wears on purpose.' She put her head slightly to one side and looked at him more closely. 'One wears a cloak, intending to hide something inside, or to keep out the cold and the rain from outside. Or both, of course. Which had you in mind?'

Hooper was taken aback. He had not expected such perception, or such candour about it. It took him a second or two to decide how to answer. 'I think he is more conscious of the threat from outside, Mrs Soames. But I don't know him; I'm basing my judgements on what other people have said. Mostly my wife, who has known him for several years, but not well, only as another parishioner.'

He saw a spark of amusement in her eyes. 'And you know someone who knows him any other way?'

That carried a wealth of possible meaning.

'The vicar was married to his sister. I imagine he knows Marlowe as well as possible,' he replied, holding her attention with his obvious sincerity.

'You put it in the past, Mr Hooper. Is she … no longer alive?' she asked. Now there was a distinct shadow in her face, the meaning of something dark, and a sadness still lingering.

Hooper did not intend to be evasive with it. 'The vicar's wife? She died some years ago.'

For the first time, she hesitated. 'In … in what manner, if I may ask? That is, if it is not confidential? I do not wish to probe.'

He wondered what trespass she was afraid of committing. What had he awakened? Was there more to Una's death than he had supposed? He found it impossible to think of Arthur Roberson in any kind of violence or deceit. If anything, he was too honest. He seemed to be vulnerability personified, the sort of man who must have an all-consuming faith to arm himself against the violence and darkness in the world, even the quiet tragedies of village life, the small sins of unkindness, indifference, the desire to dominate others and always to protect oneself; the creeping shadows of selfishness that exist anywhere there are people.

But this was too important to be covered up by the little lies of politeness that make society run smoothly. It was a comfort for which sometimes the price was too high. How should he word it? 'If you met Clementine, the young woman who is to marry Marlowe, you would like her, I think,' he began. 'And wish to protect her from making a mistake that could not be undone. And if you met Celia, my wife, I'm certain you would like her also. She is very brave, and far too perceptive, to be frank, for some people's taste. And you would understand why she is afraid for Clementine, if she marries Marlowe.'

Mrs Soames's face lit with a luminous smile. 'Then I should be pleased to meet your wife,' she replied. 'There are too few of us who are afraid of a lie more than the truth. Yes, there is a darkness in Seth Marlowe for which he wears a cloak, of sorts. And it is both inside him and outside, following behind him every step. I know no reason at all to suppose his sister, the vicar's wife, died of anything other than illness, poor woman. But Rose, his own wife, died in much darker circumstances.' She frowned.

'In the river?' He had pulled so many bodies out of the filthy, swift-moving waters of the Thames that visions came immediately to his mind. When a boat went down, and thank God that was not often, then usually all hands were lost. The tide was rapid, full of eddying currents and undertows. A woman in a long dress was like someone whose legs were bound: when the fabric filled with water, she was helpless. Above all that, the water was so polluted that it poisoned as many as it drowned.

'No,' Mrs Soames replied with a slight shake of her head.

It was a gesture so subtle that, had he not been watching her intently, he would have missed it.

'In the sea,' she finished.

'The sea?' He was startled. 'In a ship that went down? Why is that worse? And please don't deny it, your face gives you away.' That was a very personal observation, but her presence was far too intense to permit lies. Was she implying something else with this? Something even uglier than a simple tragedy? He did not know how he meant to finish the question.

'No,' she pre-empted his conclusion. 'Alone … in the water.' She met his eyes quite frankly, as if intentionally leaving him to draw his own conclusion.

'Is that all you know?'

'Yes, and also that it was one of the seaside towns on the south coast. I don't know which; it makes no difference. It was not a port, it was a beach, where people walk, some even bathe, but this was late in the day, dusk falling fast, and deserted at that time.'

She watched him, as if to see his reaction, and he was aware of it.

He waited a few moments, marshalling his thoughts, before he asked, 'What did the authorities make of it?'

'The kindest thing that could be said was that it was an accident, where the balance of her mind was turned,' she replied. 'The most unkind was that someone deliberately killed her. Possibly, they threatened her until she had nowhere to go but into the water, eventually far enough out for the tide to take her, and …'

'Was it on an outgoing tide, do you know?' he interrupted.

'So it was said,' she replied quite simply, her face showing the depth of her sadness.

'Do you believe that?' he pressed.

'I have no reason to doubt it. You can find out easily enough what the police say. I believe they concluded it was suicide, or at least that was what they called it. Of course, the coroner had to rule it so. So …' She stopped.

Hooper wanted to make her say the words, so he would not wonder afterwards if he had put them in her mouth.

'So, she did not have a Christian burial,' she concluded. 'Suicide is a sin for which you cannot repent … because there is no time left.' Her voice had not only pity, but also deep anger.

He considered if somewhere in her own life such a tragedy had happened, and the pain of it was still with her. It was a judgement that he could not go along with. Apart from anything else, it was made by men who had no idea of the agony and despair of some people's lives. Even in the best of circumstances, how could anyone judge another's pain? And who had the pitiless arrogance to wish to?

'If there is an eternity, then all of it is left,' he answered her. 'I don't know whether there is a God or not. I'd like to believe there is, and a more compassionate one than some people paint. Do we even know if it's true? Did she take her own life? If you want to judge someone, look into why.' There, he stopped himself, and with an effort. He did not even know Rose Marlowe, but he was picturing desperate unhappiness such as he had seen in the very poor, hungry, sick and possibly even homeless, people living ten, twelve, all in one room. He had been stunned by it, desperate to help and unable to. Sometimes, he longed to get away from the worst of it, anywhere that he couldn't see it.

That was one of the things Celia had given him, a place of peace where he could have the gentleness, the strength of hope, that had some base inside her and that no outside pain could destroy. He did not understand it and did not try to; it was enough that it existed.

And Clementine? Could something like that happen to her too? Had Rose Marlowe once been young and full of hope?

'You don't know,' he said. 'What about Flavia, the daughter? What happened to her?'

Mrs Soames looked downward, her face creased with unhappiness. 'I don't know. I've heard little things, but I can't say if any of them is true. Are you going to look for her? If you find her, will you let me know, please?'

Hooper thought for a moment. This was uglier than he had foreseen. Different thoughts filled his mind about Marlowe and his past, and about what had happened to Rose, and to her daughter. Had Rose got herself into deeper trouble than Marlowe had known? Than he chose to believe? Certainly, he had told no one, unless it was Roberson, who could never repeat it. Was that the source of the vicar's seemingly endless compassion for Marlowe: his knowledge of things Marlowe could not even speak of, let alone share?

So, was Clementine's compassion well placed? The giving of hope, and perhaps even happiness, in time? It mattered. Could it heal the frail future of a man who had already suffered profoundly, in a way he could not share, except with those few he could trust never to repeat it?

Hooper felt the weight of decision dark and heavy over him. What if he were wrong, hasty, following his own anger against the man because he had threatened Celia? Did he fear for Clementine, whom Celia cared for, that in an indefinite future she could end up like Marlowe's first wife, when she would be beyond anyone else's help?

'I will,' Hooper promised Mrs Soames. 'And thank you for your trust and your help.'

She smiled back at him, but there was considerable gravity in it.

Mrs Soames walked Hooper as far as the front door. She held out her hand. 'Be careful, Mr Hooper,' she said quietly. 'It's an ugly affair. There is more cruelty than either of us knows, but it is all too easy to guess.' Her face reflected helpless sorrow. 'Rose Marlowe was driven beyond what she could bear. I know only bits and pieces, but the rest lies darkly behind it. That I know for sure.'

'I am beginning to see that,' Hooper replied. 'Thank you.' He shook her hand firmly and walked away.

That evening, after his duties were finished for the day, Hooper went to the Wapping police station on the river. He hoped that William Monk, the Commander of the Thames River Police, was in his office. Hooper knew him well. He was Monk's right-hand man and they had trusted each other through many cases, both victories and disasters, and neither had ever found the other wanting. They had worked side by side with other men, and had lost some of them in tragedies that still had the power to hurt, and deeply.

Hooper walked across the dark wharf and into the building. The sun set early at this time of the year and now, at five o'clock, it was like the middle of the night. He could hear the tide lapping on the steps and slurping around the wooden pilings underneath him. The settling fog smothered all but the lights of the nearest ships riding at anchor. It was an evening to be home, but Monk was unlikely to have left yet. The air was breathtakingly cold.

Hooper pushed the door open and the warmth from the pot-bellied iron stove at the far end of the room wrapped around him immediately. There were a couple of men at their desks writing notes. He looked at Monk's office door. One of the men nodded, and Hooper walked over to it and knocked. He heard an answer and went inside.

Monk was sitting at his desk, almost clear of papers. His face was as keen as always, his grey eyes steady, but he looked tired.

'What is it?' he asked. He knew that Hooper did not interrupt him at this time of the evening without a purpose in mind.

Hooper glanced at the chair opposite the desk.

Monk nodded.

Hooper sat down, and told Monk, briefly, about Clementine. Monk already knew Celia, and admired her immensely. That fact gave Hooper a deep, abiding pleasure. Monk's respect was not easily earned, and was correspondingly valuable. He was a man with a long and dark history, and he was more than acquainted with fear: he had walked side by side with it for years. The fear he knew was not of battle, nor even of failure – they were bad enough – but the fear of his unknown past, that inner fear of memory, and all that it might contain, erased from his mind by an accident. What lay there, unquietly, waiting for the vision that unlocked the secrets of his past.

Monk's wife, Hester, before they had known each other, had gone out to the Crimea to nurse with Florence Nightingale in that catastrophic and pointless war. She was direct to a fault, brave, vulnerable in her hopes and beliefs, and when he had got to know her better, Hooper had formed a generous friendship with her. Keeping her in mind, and her often astringent and practical observations, he told Monk about his fears for Celia and her involvement with Clementine.

'Nothing I found out laid any of these fears to

rest,' he said. 'I fear Clementine is also idealistic. She is so bent on giving Marlowe the happiness that has eluded him so far that she is overlooking the possibility that his past is much darker than he has told her … or that she has imagined.'

'That he murdered Rose?' Monk was as direct as always. It was his nature to name the worst rather than creep up to it.

Hooper had said that to himself also. 'I need to know,' he said bluntly. 'He threatened Celia over the anonymous letter. Of course she didn't write it, but he believes that she did.'

'Or is using it as a weapon to keep her out of his affairs?' Monk suggested. 'One mention of a poisonous letter, with a few hints added, and someone who dislikes Celia, or is jealous of her, and the fire would be set.'

'Jealous?'

Monk smiled bleakly. 'She's a brave and honest woman, Hooper. She doesn't believe comfortable lies, and she is very perceptive. She holds the mirror straight. People see in her face what she really thinks. Not all are going to like it.'

Hooper realised with some surprise that Monk was right. Sometimes the most disturbing thing of all was the truth. It could be like a little crack in a glass, which eventually would fracture the whole thing. That was what had first drawn him to Celia, that and her courage. And although she was not traditionally beautiful, there was a grace to her he had seen in no one else.

'I'll need time to do this,' he said. 'I can't afford to wait.'

'Don't talk to me as if I'm an idiot, Hooper,' Monk said with a very slight edge of impatience. 'I can see that. When Marlowe learns you are looking into him, and he will do – you can't afford to assume he will not find out – he'll start to fight back. And he won't care who gets hurt, as long as it isn't him. Who sent the anonymous letter? Any ideas? What does Celia say?'

'Several people might have, out of spite for something or other, but she has no idea,' Hooper replied, watching Monk's face, seeing the gravity in it. 'It could be anyone,' he admitted. 'Seth Marlowe has been generous with his criticism. I don't know everyone who he has criticised, whose pride he has hurt. Or whose reputation he has damaged.'

'Will the vicar help?' Monk asked dubiously.

'I doubt it. His late wife was Marlowe's sister. He

seems to feel some obligation of care towards Marlowe. No idea what his wife might have made him promise. He is a lonely man. I think he's very fond of Clementine.'

Monk looked at him narrowly. 'I think you'd better sort this out quickly, before you have a tragedy on your hands. You need to find this daughter ... what's her name? Take the time. And a couple of men – say, Laker and Walcott – if you want them.'

'Thank you. Flavia, she's called,' Hooper replied. 'Although she may not be using it any more.' He was startled and felt a shiver of apprehension run through him. He had not expected Monk to take the matter so seriously. He was grateful ... and now genuinely afraid.

Celia was not aware of Hooper's intentions that day, but she was profoundly concerned over Clementine's future. And she was very angry indeed that Marlowe should have accused herself of writing the anonymous letter. But far more important than that, she was afraid. Who had really written it, and how many others might there be? Who else might have received one, and were they always about Marlowe? Or were they about others as well? How many people were afraid of what the postman might bring? Those three people sharing a joke a few yards away, were they laughing at her? What was true, or partly true? What were complete lies? That was the trouble with such letters: they caused fear, defence against actions that had not yet happened, and possibly never would, except for the fact that sometimes one precipitated them precisely because of that fear.

She was doing unnecessary housework because the busyness of it gave her the illusion that she was achieving something. She knew that. In the past, she had kept a beautiful house. Wood was polished until it gleamed like silk, the kitchen floor was clean enough to have been eaten from. She had been very restricted financially then, before Katherine's death and a bequest left to her, and the idea of having enough money to replace anything she wanted was still foreign to her. She had mended all sorts of things rather than spend money on new ones. She had cut worn or torn dresses into skirts, or even remade them as dresses for various children she had known to have only hand-me-downs from older siblings. Now that she had no need to do that, she still kept the habit, especially cutting down dresses for someone else to use. The sight of a little girl's face when she had a dress especially sewn for her was a reward she would not willingly give up.

Now she was working at polishing things that did not need it, because it gave her a sense of purpose, and required very little concentration. She had already peeled potatoes and chopped carrots for dinner. It was too early to slice the cabbage, and far too early to take the meat out of the cold pantry and into the warm kitchen.

Celia was pleased when the doorbell rang. She put down the duster and hurried to open it. It was nearly eleven, the perfect time to offer someone a cup of tea.

She felt differently when she saw Arthur Roberson on the step.

'Vicar! How nice to see you.' She forced herself to smile. 'Come in, please.' She stepped back and he followed after her, his smile looking as automatic as hers. 'Do you mind coming into the kitchen?' she asked. 'The fire in the sitting room isn't lit yet.'

'Of course not,' he replied. They were already at the kitchen door. 'It sounds much the better choice. No one lights a sitting-room fire this early in the day.' This was true, except for the very wealthy, or the totally idle.

She pulled out a chair for him at the kitchen table, filled the kettle and put it on the oven top, then opened the door into the fire and added a couple more pieces of coal. She poked it until the new pieces were in the heart of it, and well burning, then sat down and waited for him to speak.

He looked at her gravely, drew in breath, then seemed to change his mind. Finally, he began, and without the usual pleasantries. 'You were kind enough to tell me last Sunday how deeply you appreciated the message of my sermon. In fact, you said that it was the true meaning of Christmas. That Christ brought the possibility of forgiveness, of any and every sin, to all who would accept it. No one was shut out from that. No one at all. And no sin was excluded.' He sat perfectly still, looking straight into her eyes.

She stared back at him. He had a good face, clear and very gentle eyes, but they were also very direct, even challenging. She knew he would not be the first to look away.

She could not argue with his comment. If it was true at all, then it had to apply to everyone. 'Yes,' she said, already knowing what he was going to say next: forgive Seth Marlowe. But she was not going to say it for him.

'It is not a matter of forgiveness for past sins or mistakes; it is a prevention of future ones,' he said quietly. 'It's usually easy to forgive those we like,' he went on. 'Really forgiving and forgetting those offences committed by those we don't like, that's hard.' He shook his head very fractionally. 'I do not ask you to like Seth Marlowe, my dear, or to stop caring for Clementine.' He hesitated. 'But if you can forgive him for her sake, this marriage is a chance of happiness for both of them.' He smiled. 'And happiness is very healing. I think you know that for yourself?'

That was a comment that went straight to its mark. She was happy, totally happy, with John Hooper. It was as if the sun had risen and a bright light shone on her whole world. Certainly, there was still pain in it, there were battles to be fought, work to do, selfishness and thoughtlessness to be overcome, but there was a joy through all of it that gave meaning and life to it. She found herself smiling even at the thought.

'I read the answer to that in your face, my dear,'

Roberson said gently. 'Would you deny that to Clementine? She is not at fault, whatever you think of Seth.'

He left the question hanging as to whether she thought Seth would bring happiness, or imprisoning grief to Clementine. But could she say that to him? Wasn't that the very sort of judgement she deplored in others?

As if he had read her thoughts, he spoke, and his response was not quite the one she had been imagining. 'If John Hooper's friends had said to him that he should not marry a woman who would lie on the witness stand, for any reason at all, would you have expected him to listen, and withdraw his offer to you?'

She had done it to save Hooper's life! Did Roberson not understand that? 'It was to …' she began.

'… to save Hooper's life,' he finished for her. 'I know, but other people don't. They might judge differently.'

'They have no right—' she started to say.

'Of course they haven't,' he agreed. 'That was rather my point.'

She felt the heat rise up her face. She had not expected such a powerful argument from Arthur

Roberson, intellectually or morally. A part of her was pleased, and a part of her was angry that Clementine had chosen Marlowe to marry, and not Arthur Roberson. No, that was not fair! Marlowe had asked her, Roberson had not. And he was desperately lonely. That she knew as profoundly as she knew anything.

No, that was stupid of her! Perhaps he *had* asked Clementine and she had refused him. Why might she? Could it have been that she did not wish to be in Una's shadow, because he had loved her? Seth Marlowe may once have loved Rose, but he had turned that to hatred, even revulsion, a long time ago.

She was speculating and she had no idea. That was the sort of partial assumption she deplored.

'What about the letter?' she asked. 'Who wrote it? And why? He thinks it was me! And he has promised to hurt John if it happens again. I have no control over that because I didn't write it, and I have no idea who did. I can't prevent that person from writing such a letter again ... and again ... to anyone.'

'I've spent a lot of time on my knees about that,' he said gravely.

'I suppose God can stop people doing such things,

but he can't take the wickedness out of their hearts, can he?' she asked, and heard the bitterness and confusion in her voice. 'Wouldn't that, in effect, rob us of ever being either good or bad?'

'I don't know,' he replied. 'Perhaps. But I wasn't asking Him to. I only asked for guidance as to what I should do.'

She swallowed hard. 'And what do you think that is going to be?'

'I don't know, but I'm afraid of it. I think it won't be anything I wish to do, or else I would have thought of it for myself.' That was devastating honesty.

'You think that He would answer you?' It was a serious question. Did Arthur Roberson really believe that God literally answered such questions?

'Oh, yes.' He sounded rueful. 'I will know ... if I want to.'

She hesitated only a moment 'Don't you want to?'

'No, because I think it will be something decisive, and I'd dread it.' The shadow of a smile crossed his face. 'The only thing worse is living with the guilt afterwards. Uncertainty is corrosive, you know. Whatever happens, you always wonder if the alternative would have been better somehow.'

'And what should I do? Will God tell me that?' she asked.

'I think He already has. Be gentle with Clementine. Don't add to her loneliness by blaming her for choosing to marry Marlowe. I know that what he says is unreasonable, and worse than that, it is selfish, born out of his fear that he would lose her, if she listens to you.'

That was good sense, and Celia knew it. She did not argue.

'And the letter?' he asked.

She considered that for a moment. 'I find it very difficult to put up with her believing that I wrote it.'

'She doesn't,' he answered quickly. 'And I know it is vile. I don't know who did write it, and I have made as many enquiries as I dare without explaining what it is, which is precisely what the writer wishes, I think.'

She did not tell him that she had spoken of the letter to Hooper, and asked him to find the source – or enough information so that she could decide what to do about it when that time came, if it ever did.

'You must forgive Seth, however hard you find it,' Roberson continued, leaning forward a little. 'You do not know if he has repented of anything of which he was guilty, or if his misery is only the pain and grief of losing his first wife and his daughter, his only child. That must hurt him every day, and—'

'He blames Rose,' Celia cut in. 'He says so, every time he mentions her.'

'I know. Perhaps that is something yet to heal, and Clementine may help him more than you or I can grasp. It is a wonderful thing to be loved, Celia. I think you and I both know that.'

That cut deep inside her. It was wonderful to look into Hooper's face in an unguarded moment, to see the light and the gentleness in his eyes, for her to see him sit at ease in his own home, her home – their home – and see his hand resting on the arm of the chair, uncurled, completely at ease for her to feel the warmth fill her, too, and the gratitude. She could not wish anyone harm in those moments. Roberson was right: to accept that for oneself and deny it to others touched the borders of the unforgivable. 'Yes,' she said. 'I wish that for Clementine, of course I do. And it would be wicked to deny it to anyone, even Seth Marlowe.'

'The kettle is boiling,' he told her, looking beyond her at the plume of steam rising from the stove.

'Oh, of course!' She rose to her feet. 'I'll make tea.'

But it was not as easy as it had seemed when agreeing with Arthur Roberson. Early the following afternoon, she had another visitor, and this time it was Seth Marlowe. The moment she saw his face, she knew the encounter was going to be difficult. His eyes were blazing beneath his heavy brows, and his mouth was pulled into a thin, angry line. He did not wait to be invited in, but reached his arm above hers and pushed the door open, walking straight in past her.

She was about to protest, but the words died on her lips. She closed the front door and followed him across the hall and into the sitting room. He stood in the middle of the carpet with a paper in his hand. He held it high and shook it. 'Swear to me that you didn't write this one either!' His voice was already shrill and rising. 'Have you no shame, woman?'

Celia felt cold right through to her bones. So, it had come, another letter.

He leaned forward a little. 'Admit it! You wrote this.' He shook the paper until it rattled. 'You … you …' He seemed lost for words sufficiently damning.

'I did not!' She raised her own voice to match his pitch and anger. 'I don't know what it says, but perhaps if you get hold of your temper and use your brain, we might work out who actually did. Or are you afraid of that, because you know?'

'I already know, you stupid creature! It was you. You are a pathetic, jealous woman!' he shouted. 'Well, I won't give in to you! I'll show this to Clementine, and we'll see if she wants to see you or speak to you ever again!'

Celia was shaking with fury, and fear. Suddenly, a friendship she had valued for years looked as if it were coming to a miserable end. How could this man really love Clementine if he denied her any friends, expected her to change her whole life, cut herself off from anyone he didn't like, fairly or not? The chaos and the cruelty of his having total control of someone else's life shook Celia's belief in any sort of certainty. She must steady her mind, think clearly. She couldn't give in to such bullying. But what could she do? Looking at Marlowe, and then the letter, she saw the reason for his fear – and it was fear, really. This rage was springing from his fear of losing something he valued very much. She knew that, even if she doubted the reason for it. It was not out of consideration for Clementine's feelings, of that she was perfectly sure.

Marlowe took a step towards her. If he reached forward now, he would touch her.

It galvanised her to life. 'You think I wrote this? Why? You already threatened me, and I told you I would not see Clementine if it was going to endanger her happiness.' Actually, she could not remember what she had said, but stating it now might help. 'I care how she feels, which you clearly do not. And if my staying away from her is for the better – so long as she knows it is your order that keeps me away and not my own choice, or any change in my friendship for her – then I would keep my word.'

He relaxed a fraction, but his knuckles where he held the letter were clenched and white, and only a few feet from her face.

'The letter you told me of was cruel, and accused you of being the cause of your first wife's death. What does this one say?'

'As if you didn't know!' he said between his teeth.

'I don't! And, personally, I don't care. But if you want to stop them you'd better discover who wrote it before they start writing them to other people as well. I suppose they haven't done that yet? Are you sure?'

He froze, horror making his mouth gape open.

'Then you'd better find out,' she said with as much self-control as she could manage. 'It's the only way to stop them. And soon, before they start sending them all over the place.'

He wavered.

'Think!' she ordered. 'Who has reason to want to hurt you?'

'Only you.'

'I could name three others at least,' she retorted. 'Perhaps it would narrow it down if you could say who knew the information in the letter. I presume it must be a very small number of people, since telling everybody isn't a threat worth bothering with, if they already know.'

'It's lies, you … you stupid woman!' He almost spat the words.

She kept her temper with increasing difficulty. 'About what? About whom? I'm trying to narrow it down, so you can at least rule out some. I take it you do want to stop them?'

He was silent for a moment, then he realised that

she was right. She saw the change in his eyes. 'I don't know. It's wicked inventions about how my wife died, and the circumstances leading up to it. Accusations about our marriage … It's … cruel. It hurts me, and if it gets to be known, it would hurt Clementine terribly.'

For a moment she was actually sorry for him. Happiness was sometimes so fragile, and so precious. 'Is there anything in it that has reference to something private? If so, that would rule out most of us. You didn't live here then, and I've never heard you speak of that time. Think about it.'

'Only Arthur Roberson,' he said slowly.

She was stunned. 'For heaven's sake, if you think he would do that, you're crazy! Why? What on earth would make him stoop to such a base and wicked thing?'

'Clementine,' he said slowly.

'Rubbish!' She was really angry.

'You haven't seen—' he began.

'No, I haven't, and neither have you!'

'Oh, but I have.' He said it firmly, quite sure of himself. 'He may not even have admitted it to himself, but he's in love with Clementine. He wants her. And she has chosen me.' He stood a little straighter, but still too close. 'Thank you, Mrs Hooper, I think you have hit the nail on the head. Arthur knows all about me. His wife was my sister. He acts as if he has forgiven me for my wife's death, but in his heart he blames me. He can't accept what she was. Una refused to believe it either. It all fits together.'

'No! Arthur has been the one person who has always defended you!' she protested. 'That's a wicked suggestion and completely untrue.'

'You are naïve, Mrs Hooper. You think a clerical collar makes a man innocent, but it can also mask a multitude of sins. It is the best disguise in the world. But masks can be torn off.' He started to walk round her towards the door.

'You were wrong about me,' she said loudly, 'and you are wrong about him, too.'

'No, I'm not! I'm obliged to you.' He opened the door into the hall. 'I can put an end to this.'

She followed after him, almost on his heels. 'If you accuse the vicar of writing those letters, you'll be wrong. And you will make an enemy not only of a good man who's defended you all the time you've been here, but you will make an enemy of just about everyone in this community, including Clementine!'

'Of you, perhaps, but your judgement was never

much good. Most of the rest of them, when they realise I am right, and they are wrong, will be revolted, and—'

'They won't believe you. Unless you show them the letters, of course.' She saw him flinch and went on. 'Are you prepared to do that? And let them judge between you and Arthur Roberson? Well, are you? Also, you accused me wrongly and called me a liar. You haven't apologised for that yet.'

'Perhaps you put him up to it?' Marlowe raised his eyebrows, as if he actually could believe what he said.

Celia was so astonished that she was rooted to the spot and he was at the front door before she could even think to reply. He opened it and stepped outside into the dark, slamming it behind him. She drew in her breath, but the only words that came to her mind were ones she had heard in her head, but had never actually said aloud. She was ashamed even to think them.

Hooper set out the next morning. He walked briskly to the ferry and took it downriver as far as Wapping Stairs and the police station. It cost extra, but it was worth it. He paid the ferryman and went up the wet and slippery stone steps on to the wharf, and across to the police station door. With Monk's permission, two men, Laker and Walcott, were to assist him. He was profoundly grateful for them. With these men to help, and the convenience of having use of one of the station's boats, it would be simple to row upriver and moor at the steps nearest their destination. Hooper found an ease and a familiarity on the water, and would even more so with these men by his side.

Laker and Walcott were waiting and the three of them left immediately. They were well into their rowing before the men spoke.

'What are we looking for when we get there?' asked Laker.

'Any information about Seth Marlowe, or his wife, Rose, or their daughter, Flavia. She may not be using that name. We don't know a lot about her, only that she has, or used to have, auburn hair.'

Time passed, and it took considerable effort to row against the ebb tide, before Hooper continued, 'Marlowe has lived in several different places in the past, but was a regular churchgoer. What we know about Rose is that she died by drowning, not in the river, but in the sea, off the south coast. Their daughter, Flavia, is still alive. Or … we think she is.'

'If she is, do we know where she might be living?' asked Walcott. 'Or of someone else who was closely involved with any of them?'

Hooper shook his head. It was cold this morning and he needed his strength to keep the boat moving. He felt the beginning of the incoming tide to help them.

Everything was grey, except where the clouds broke and the sun shone on the water's face in brief moments of silver. The dark hulls of ships at anchor had a strange beauty about their old wood, barnacle-crusted below the waterline. Some were wide-bellied for cargo, others sleek for speed. Tall masts rose into the sky and barely moved in the early-morning stillness.

It had been a hard night and he had not slept well. He had known the moment he went in through his front door that Celia was distressed, although it was a while before she told him what had happened, and longer still before he realised what had upset her the most. Apparently, Marlowe had arrived in a raging temper, waving another anonymous letter in his bony hand. She could not say exactly what was in it because he had not let her read it. Again, however, he had outlined the content and accused her of having written it.

When Celia related how she had countered not with fear, but with intelligent questions as to who could have had the information contained in it, Hooper was relieved. She explained that, after a moment's thought, Marlowe had announced that only the vicar, Arthur Roberson, had known all the facts and could easily have made up the few he had not known. What had distressed Celia so much was that Roberson was now a suspect. In fact, he was now the only one, and Celia herself had caused that to happen. She was weighed down by guilt, but even worse than that, by the fear that other people might believe it, and that Roberson would be despised, possibly even driven out.

Had he not been so distressed for Celia, Hooper would have been enraged himself by such a terrible injustice. Whatever reason would the vicar have for doing such a thing? Celia had told him the same moment he realised it for himself: Clementine, of course. He had seen the way Roberson looked at her; he had heard the tenderness in his voice.

Or was Marlowe seeing the vicar as a rival, and

doing this himself to drive Roberson out? No, that was too convoluted. Anyway, Roberson had not asked Clementine to marry him, Marlowe had. And Hooper could not imagine Roberson stooping to the level of writing poisonous letters to Marlowe, anonymously or not. It was Hooper's profession to judge a man's intentions and always to pursue guilt. Was he so bad at it that he had seen the guilt in Marlowe, and not in Roberson? Somebody had written the letters, although it seemed that no one had read them except Marlowe himself. Apparently, they contained references to Marlowe's behaviour during his marriage, before he came to the village: things Roberson might know, in the utmost secrecy and confidence. But who else would have known? Hooper racked his mind to think of all possibilities. Who had known Una? Wasn't that Roberson's dead wife's name? Who might she have told, if Rose had confided in her? After all, they were sisters-in-law.

He had asked Celia, and had seen the sudden understanding in her eyes. Hooper had expected her to mention someone in the village, but she had stumbled over the words when she answered.

'Me!' she had told him. 'She talked a lot to me

when I was looking after her in her last months. She didn't tell me anything about Seth, but I suppose, from his point of view, she could have. That's why Marlowe thought it was me! Only now he is sure it is Arthur. What can we do?'

The tears had been running down her face as she spoke. And he had no answer.

He did not pretend. He entertained the idea for a few moments, and discarded it. They had never lied to each other. He would destroy something infinitely precious if he did now. And he should not discuss with her the idea that Roberson had a darker side, which he had not seen, not even a shadow of it in the brief time he had known him. But he thought again of what Celia had said of Roberson's impassioned plea for repentance and forgiveness. Was that all theoretical, or did some dark pain hide behind and within his words? Can anyone plead so intensely for something they had no need of themselves?

It was a rhetorical question. He knew the answer. Of course, Roberson felt guilt over something, every honest man did. And whether it was large or small was not the point. Even a single grain of sand, when it was in the eye, can be exquisitely painful. Had

Celia caught that, too, and wondered if Marlowe could be right?

Hooper and the men were making good time. They had rowed in unison with silent understanding for years now: the fair-haired, ambitious Laker, with his handsome face and the impudent air hiding his dreams; the darker, stockier Walcott, who spoke so little and seldom showed any emotion. Hooper understood them both. They had tested each other's courage through many dangers, and a few tragedies. Words were an unnecessary disturbance of the rhythm.

Hooper returned to his own thoughts as his arms automatically pulled at the oars. Marlowe had said he had confided in the vicar. Who did the vicar confide in? And in asking that question, Hooper had a sudden glimpse of the vast loneliness of a man who believed that God had set him aside to be a refuge for others, someone to whom they could trust to speak the truth, to judge fairly, to offer God's forgiveness for certain offences or, in time, for all of them. Without anyone to assure him when he was right, and tell him gently when they thought he was mistaken. If Roberson had indeed loved Clementine, why had he not asked her to marry him? Or was he moving towards it too slowly, and Marlowe had beaten him to it?

There was no answer to any of these questions, only more questions. He did not have to tell Celia otherwise. After she had told him of the meeting with Marlowe, he had simply brushed the stray lock of hair off her brow, where it was coming out of its pins, then taken her in his arms. It was not an answer, but it was an intense, wordless comfort. He had held her even closer, and felt her relax, leaning against him a little, calmer, turning her head sideways to rest against his cheek.

Silence and touch were infinitely better than words of comfort that were not true, and promises you could not keep.

There was silence now apart from the sound of the water lapping against the sides of the boat. They were more than halfway to the steps closest to their destination. They were past the warehouses and shipyards, beginning to pass residential areas.

His thoughts were interrupted by Laker's voice. 'Sorry?'

'I asked you what he's done, this Marlowe,' said Laker. 'It might help if we knew that.'

'Fair question,' Hooper replied. 'He's a self-righteous prig who goes to church every Sunday and tells people what is wrong with them, and what they should do about it.' He saw both men frown. 'He's been getting anonymous letters,' he went on. 'And I want to know who sent them.'

'Why?' Walcott asked. 'Sounds like he deserved them.'

Hooper held up a finger. 'One, because the vicar is being blamed for it, and I don't think he's at fault.' He put up a second finger. 'Two, I want to know exactly what's in them, and if it's true.' He put up a third finger. 'At the moment, my wife is also being blamed.' He raised his fourth finger. 'And this man is about to marry a very nice young woman whose loyalty he will test to the last degree by cutting her off from all her friends.'

'What did those letters say?' Laker asked.

Hooper smiled. Laker always wanted to know everything. 'The second one implied that he more or less drove his wife to suicide. The first one, I don't know. Whether there was anything more or not, he kept it to himself. I'd like to know how much of that is an exaggeration by someone who hates him and how much of it is true. Does that help?'

'Yes, sir,' Laker answered with a grin. 'A pleasure, sir.'

Hooper gave them the rest of the information he had; specifically, what Mrs Soames had said.

Laker lifted his hand from the oar and rubbed his eyes. 'Families,' he said with a downturn of his mouth.

Hooper did not comment. He knew Laker, and his dreams, and tragedies.

Walcott said nothing.

They arrived at the steps to the Pimlico pier and secured the boat. As they stretched against muscles made tight from the exertion, Hooper gave them instructions where to begin their search.

'This is the last place he lived in, according to what he told Roberson. He will have attended church, because it is the one place where he feels comfortable. There will be churchgoers about this morning. Ask until you find someone who knew him. Hear all you can. He's bound to have made enemies. He's a compulsive preacher, always telling people what they ought to be doing, and what they ought not. We'll meet back at the pier at four. You take inland, Laker. Use an omnibus if you need to. You take the east, Walcott. I'll take the west.'

'I don't suppose he'd go to a pub?' Laker asked with a twisted smile.

'Neither do I,' Hooper agreed. 'If he drank at all, it would be alone. But he likes to have an audience. Someone to tell how they should live. Try any societies that sound likely. Nothing frivolous ...'

'God help us,' Laker said sourly. 'Is this girl really going to marry him?' A flash of pity lit his face.

'Maybe she's desperate?' Walcott suggested, leaving the exact meaning of his remark unsaid.

'She will be a lot more, if she goes ahead with it,' Laker answered.

'Then get on with finding out all you can about him,' Hooper ordered. 'Somebody hates him enough to write him poisonous letters.'

The first place Hooper called was the church in the neighbourhood where Marlowe had lived before moving to Soames's parish. That corresponded, as far as he could tell, with the time Rose Marlowe had died, roughly six years ago. He considered visiting the vicar, but what could the man tell him, even if he was willing? Only that Rose had drowned. Anything personal that he knew would be in confidence, and no clergyman of any denomination would break his vows of silence to tell a casual questioner, even from the police, anything that would be of help. Better to go straight to the police.

It was a little after ten o'clock when he walked in the door of the local police station and across the dusty floor to the desk. He spoke to the sergeant on duty, introducing himself, giving his rank, and adding that he was working directly with Commander Monk of the Thames River Police. That might catch the man's attention.

'Morning, sir,' the sergeant responded. 'How can I help you?'

'It is concerning a death some six or seven years ago, a drowning, but not in the river. In the sea, off the south coast, I believe. But the woman who died lived in your area.'

'In the sea, you say?' The sergeant looked puzzled.

'Yes. Before I take a train all the way to the coast, I'd like to know something about her and her husband.' He saw the man's face begin to reflect a certain anxiety. 'What has reopened the issue is a matter of anonymous letters,' he added.

The sergeant's nose wrinkled, as if he smelled something sour.

'Very nasty,' Hooper went on.

'Coward's way,' the sergeant agreed. 'Usually find

it's a woman. Good with words, they are. How can we help?'

Hooper did not have time to be subtle. Unless he was very lucky, this would be a long and fruitless trail. A lot of people could be hurt while he was going in the wrong direction, even when treading carefully. 'The woman who died was named Rose Marlowe.' He saw the sergeant's mouth turn down and a slight shake of his head. 'Unpleasant things are being suggested about her death,' Hooper went on. 'Innocent people could be hurt. But regardless of that, poisonous letters are a crime, when there's a threat in them. And libellous, if the accusations aren't true. Of course, it's a crime if they are! Possibly murder.'

He was exaggerating to some extent. As far as he knew, there was no suggestion of that. But how much *did* he know? Only what Celia had told him of Marlowe's rage and, she thought, also fear. And what about the next letter, and the one after that? He may be slipping ahead of events, but not very far ahead! It would be too late to be sorry afterwards.

'Poor woman,' the sergeant said simply. 'They said it was suicide. But I suppose you know that? Dreadfully unhappy she was, poor creature.'

'How do you know that?' Hooper asked quickly.

Perhaps this man could give him something new to follow up, new ideas, new feelings.

'It isn't only the River Police that's good at their jobs,' the sergeant said, lifting his chin a little, his voice a note sharper. 'See things as you can't interfere with. Like to stop it, but you can't. You can catch some fellows easy enough, but not the respectable ones, specially churchgoers, like. Hide behind a smart suit and a clean collar and get all the grammar right, and you can't touch them.'

'Don't go round and round the bushes, man!' Hooper kept his patience with difficulty. 'Do you mean her husband?'

'Course I do. Although he might have said different.'

'You mean they had a violent sort of relationship? And no matter how much you might have disliked Marlowe, nothing except the truth is any good to me.'

The sergeant started to answer, then changed his mind. He remained silent for a few moments, then spoke more carefully. 'Mrs Marlowe never said anything herself, and of course it didn't happen where other people could see it.' He shook his head. 'But other women see, you know? My wife told me when she met Mrs Marlowe at the grocer's, or the butcher's, with her face all bruised, like, and covered up with face powder, or an arm it hurt her to use. Marge liked Mrs Marlowe, and she said to me more than once that we should do something about it. But what can we do? The law doesn't say a man can't chastise his wife, if he thinks she needs it, God help her.'

Hooper felt a chill run through him, as if the wind had changed. 'You think it was him?'

'I know it was,' the sergeant said in disgust. 'Seen the fear in her eyes. She would've said if it were anyone else. And anyway, that girl of hers, Flora or something like that, she said right out it were her father what did that.'

'Did you speak to her about it?' Hooper asked.

The sergeant gave him a contemptuous look. 'And say what? Only get the woman beaten again, and likely enough the daughter, too.'

'What happened to the daughter when her mother died?'

The sergeant's face creased with sorrow. 'Proper cut up, she was. Went a bit doolally. Then took to the streets to live, poor little thing! Pretty, she was. I expect she will do all right for five or ten years, till someone beats the hell out of her, or she gets some disease or other. I hope he rots in hell. And I won't apologise for saying so.'

Hooper tried to keep the emotion out of his own voice, but it was difficult. 'Who would hate him enough to write anonymous letters to him?' He had never seen Flavia, if that was indeed her name, but Clementine's bright face kept coming to his mind. How could she bear it if she had a child, and it were abused? Would the village help her? Or would they turn a blind eye, and walk past, finding any excuse not to interfere? Of course, this charge could be wrong. The letters must be stopped. They could do terrible damage with their suspicions. Rose Marlowe might have been as mentally unstable as Marlowe himself said. Flavia could have taken her mother's part for any number of reasons, from actual observation of violence to a vengeance against her father for what she had seen, or been told by her mother – truths, partial truths or outright lies, to protect a lover, or anything else. Or perhaps Flavia, like anyone else, did not wish to believe that her mother was very seriously deranged.

Still, murder could not be ruled out. That was enough to frighten anyone.

It made sense of Marlowe's behaviour, as Hooper had seen it. But it was only one view. It was word of mouth, hearsay, not evidence.

'Can you give me the name of the vicar of the church he went to?' he asked the sergeant. And when the sergeant wrote it down for him, he asked for other names as well: a doctor, her neighbours, local tradesmen she would have dealt with.

'Are you going to do something, sir?' The sergeant's voice lifted with hope.

'I'm going to find as much as I can of the truth, and that has to include who wrote those letters. A lot of damage can be done to the innocent, as well as the guilty,' Hooper replied. It was an evasion and he knew it.

'Innocent?' the sergeant asked. 'I thought you said they were written to him.'

'You know the man. Do you suppose he takes them quietly and burns them in the grate?' Hooper asked. 'He has twice accused my wife of having written them, and forbidden her to remain friends with the young woman he is going to marry. If she doesn't obey him, he has threatened to misinterpret an event in her recent past, which I am aware of – I was there – until all the people in the community know about it. But lies …' He stopped when he saw the expression on the man's face. 'I'll do what I can,' he finished quietly. 'Thank you.'

The sergeant wrote half a dozen names and addresses on a sheet of paper and passed it across the desk to Hooper. 'Look after your wife, sir. And if you can find the girl, maybe you could do something for her?'

'I will.' It was a promise.

Hooper spoke first to the neighbours. Most of them said very little, but whether it was because they knew little or there was little to repeat, he was not sure. A picture emerged that fitted into what he already knew. Seth Marlowe was an easy man to dislike. He was outspoken, critical, self-righteous. But he was also rigorously honest, paying all his bills on time, and on occasion he was even generous. His manner was stiff, but always polite. He did not report gossip or repeat it, and he never lied.

The churchgoers among them also said that Marlowe spoke of forgiveness, but only after confession was given and repentance was proved. Perhaps the thing that Hooper felt most deeply was that Marlowe apparently had no sense of humour. Life had been hard for him. Certainly, Hooper knew from Roberson that Rose had brought him a deep and understandable grief, shame and, ultimately, bereavement. That was a wound that would take years to heal, if it ever did.

Reluctantly, Hooper could understand why the fear of losing Clementine – with her courage, her bright face, love of life, happy laughter and, above that, her trust – all cut so deeply it threatened everything that mattered to Marlowe, his safety of mind and of heart.

As he spoke to people, Hooper found only suggestions, memories that were painful but conflicted. He saved them to mull over later, when he was home.

He met up with Laker and Walcott at a little after four and they climbed into the boat. The men took him back to the stairs nearest his home, along the way telling him what little they had found. It added weight to what he already knew, and confirmed Marlowe's reputation for interfering. Apparently, Walcott had found out, he had been considered quite an authority about history, beginning with the Reformation. Laker had found a doctor who had treated Rose Marlowe. He was grieved and angry, but he would tell them no details, although he was not surprised to learn that she was dead.

Hooper thanked them. 'See you tomorrow. Good night.'

''Night, sir!' they replied above the slurping of the water on the stone steps leading up to the quayside.

The first thing Hooper did, as soon as he came through the door, was to see that it was closed and locked behind him, barring the night where the heavy wind was carrying an edge of sleet. Celia came out of the sitting room the moment she heard the latch fall, her face creased with concern. He could see that it was for him, that she saw he was cold and tired, but more for the distress he might be feeling.

He hugged her first, before saying anything. Wordless comfort was what he needed, before even trying to tell her what he had found, and what he had not. She seemed to understand the need for explanation. Perhaps that was what love ought to be, what home now meant, whether it was geographically or in the pattern of your life. He ate a whole dish of stew before she asked him what he had learned.

He hesitated. He thought of omitting some of the darker facts, but lying to her would hurt her more. And he wanted to share the weight of it, perhaps selfishly. 'Apparently Marlowe hasn't changed,' he began. 'He – according to those who knew them – he actually beat her.' He watched the shock, and then the disgust in her face.

'It is more common than you might think,' she said very quietly. 'Women don't report it. Some are convinced it is their fault. They don't want other people to know. And anyway, where would they go?'

'Thank God he isn't a real vicar! There's none of the … mercy … the caring that Arthur Roberson has.' He hesitated only a moment. 'And it seems it has been there a long time.'

'Arthur won't stand up against him,' she said reluctantly. 'I don't know why, but I presume it has something to do with some promise he might have made to Una. Maybe she protected Seth because he was her brother. Family loyalty. Or perhaps she really did know something we don't.'

He hesitated a moment, then said what he was thinking. 'Or perhaps Roberson just evaded conflict.'

Celia's face was full of concern. She looked down for a moment.

Hooper waited silently.

She looked up again, her eyes reflecting her deep

distress. 'Or perhaps Marlowe is blackmailing him over something, as he tried to do to me. Perhaps there was something in Una's death, an error, or an act of mercy misplaced, that makes Arthur defend him, whatever the truth is.' She breathed in and out again, slowly. 'Arthur has no one to turn to. He knows a lot of secrets of a lot of people. And he will be bound to protect anyone who has trusted him.'

Hooper had not even thought of that. 'Oh God!' he whispered. 'What a burden to carry. He might know the truth, or a lot more of it, but be unable to tell us, even to hint at anything. Thank God I'm not a priest! What an unbearable load to carry!'

'Perhaps you would have to trust God to sort it out somehow?' Celia said, her face creased with worry.

'Does He do that?' Hooper asked, then wished he had not. It was a question that probed the depth of her faith. But it was impossible to take back.

She gave a brief smile. 'God won't fix it,' she answered. 'But He'll show somebody else how to.'

'You mean one of us?'

She put out her hand and he grasped it.

'Probably,' she agreed.

*

Next morning, Hooper went first to the River Police station at Wapping, on the north bank of the river, and learned that Walcott had found an address where Marlowe had lived before the one Soames gave to Hooper. But an investigation into it revealed nothing new that appeared to have meaning. Apparently, Seth Marlowe had always been a profound believer, and a judgemental man. He had considered finding and naming fault to be a pastoral care. He had never realised that more often than not it brought out the defensiveness in people, and it very seldom made anything better.

On the other hand, he gave generously of both his time and his means. No one doubted that, and some were genuinely grateful. A few even pitied him for having such a joyless wife, and then a painfully wayward daughter.

The letters were key, Hooper told Laker and Walcott, who had no major cases that required their attention, just petty robberies that anyone could handle. Two days away would make little difference, and Monk had made it clear he could foresee all the tragedies that would happen if any more letters were sent to Seth Marlowe, and he blamed anyone who was innocent.

'Do you know exactly what the letters said, sir?' Laker asked. 'Like exactly? Might give us the chance to ...'

'No,' Hooper replied. 'Actually, he didn't make a complaint, although, as I told you, he accused my wife of having written the first. And then he came to our home and accused her of writing the second. Then, she told me, he suddenly broke off and started accusing the vicar of writing the letters. But he didn't apologise to her for his appalling behaviour.'

'Don't suppose he sees apologising as necessary,' Walcott said drily. 'But you reckon he thinks the vicar really wrote the letters?'

'That's what I'm afraid of, and that he's going to settle it himself,' Hooper admitted. 'I don't think he's right, though.'

'But whoever did write them, they've got it coming to them,' Laker retorted. 'Filthy thing. Coward's way ...'

'For the moment, it's the only way,' Hooper pointed out. 'If you have no power, no money, no position, and nobody would believe you against a pillar of righteousness like Seth Marlowe ...'

'You mean a woman, or a servant, someone dependent?' Laker asked.

'Well, it shouldn't be like that,' Hooper agreed. 'But …'

'You trying to upend the whole of society, and start again?' Laker asked with a crooked smile. 'Wherever you start, before you got halfway, they've gone right back again to masters and servants, bullies and victims, those that have and those who have not. Begging your pardon, sir, but you know nothing at all!'

'I'm not trying to move up in society. I'm trying to find out who wrote anonymous letters to Seth Marlowe before he gets to them – or to who he thinks it is – before there's a real physical crime and someone is badly hurt,' Hooper replied tartly.

The smile vanished from Laker's face and the growing amusement from Walcott's also.

'Yes, sir,' Laker said. 'Should I be looking at women in particular? Like a friend of his wife who died? Or at any man who cared about her? Did she have family?'

'No, and I thought of that,' Hooper replied. 'She had no particular friends. Perhaps if she had, they might have helped her when she was alive.' He heard the anger in his own voice and realised he cared very much about what had happened to Rose Marlowe. Was he believing the worst about Seth Marlowe because he did not like the man? He barely knew him. That was simple. He had verbally attacked Celia, and Hooper believed that he was already bullying Clementine and asserting control over her that could only get worse. Was he being careful and perceptive, preventing a wrong before it happened? Or being unjust to a man he did not like? Overprotective of a woman he loved more and more deeply as time passed? And protective of Clementine because Celia cared for her?

'We have to find who wrote those letters and what was in them,' he stated.

'Well, you said there were no postmarks, sir,' Walcott began. 'So delivered by hand, they were. Someone who knows where he lives and can get there easily, and nobody notices them.'

'Yes, it has to be somebody who knows a good deal about him that isn't general knowledge,' Hooper agreed. 'I couldn't trace any friends like that. But then, I suppose no one would be likely to admit it, especially if they had written the letters.'

'You didn't see the letters yourself at all, sir? I mean … even the handwriting?' Laker asked.

'No,' Hooper admitted. 'But I believe they're real. Marlowe's anger wasn't assumed. He was almost hysterical with rage. And I presume they caused fear, which means there was something in them that he was afraid of. We can't ask his wife, poor woman. There's no use asking a church vicar who might know or might not, but either way he can't tell us.'

'What about this daughter, sir?' Laker asked. 'If we find her, she might know a lot.'

'If she's taken to the streets, poor little thing, good luck finding her,' Walcott said bitterly. 'She'll be invisible by now. And she won't be calling herself Marlowe!' His face was creased with sudden, fierce anger, as if he were imagining her as a child of his own.

'You reckon it's all to do with his wife, sir?' Laker asked. 'Only it's maybe something she did that would reflect badly on him? Or worse, maybe make him a laughing stock? Nobody likes to look ridiculous. Laugh *with* him might be fine, but laugh *at* him is another thing altogether. Specially to a self-righteous man like that, with a huge sense of self-importance, and none of humour.'

'Exactly,' Hooper replied. 'And we don't always know which things are sensitive to someone. We really need to find the daughter.'

'If she's still alive,' Walcott put in. 'She was in the right place, and would know if the stories are true. Street life is miserable for young girls, especially if they aren't very streetwise—'

'I know,' Hooper cut him off. He had seen this for himself. Too many of them were found eventually in the river. Even one was too many.

They took out a map, divided the areas between them, according to the bits and pieces of information they had, and the informants they knew who might be able to tell them something. Mrs Soames's rough description of Flavia as having auburn hair was all they had to go on. But perhaps that would help?

And if he found her, what then? Would she have any idea who wrote those letters? The events they referred to almost certainly dated back to before her mother died, and she herself had left home. She might know who else was aware of their circumstances then. But even if she did, would she tell anyone, particularly a man from the River Police?

Hooper could think of nothing more to help, and he was compelled to protect Celia from Marlowe's anger and possible revenge. What was in the letters that drove him to such fury?

He returned to the area that Marlowe had lived in

before he had arrived at the Reverend Mr Soames's church. It was roughly opposite Celia's house, but on the north side of the river, where the main port of the city was. He had read that London was the biggest city in the world. He was more acquainted with the fact that the Pool of London was the biggest dock.

There was much good about his years at sea. He had seen sights that stretched his mind, and lit his imagination. They gave him an awe and respect for life in all its forms, human and otherwise. For the variety of it, the wit, above all the beauty. But now he was glad to return to his home every night, to see the same pathway to the door, the flowers in the garden, the roses, in particular the yellow ones, and above all, to have Celia welcome him. Perhaps he valued it more than those who had always had a home and took it for granted?

What had Marlowe had … and then lost?

Flavia.

It took him most of that day and the one after to find her, with help from both Laker and Walcott. The local police station could be of little help, except to say that her name was known, but they were reluctant to press any charges against her. She was very young, and only just getting by. One of the local charities helped her now and then. No one had claimed she had robbed them. Generally, the police used prostitutes for information, and pretty much left them alone. None of them knew much about her, except it was thought that she had auburn hair, like her mother.

They visited local brothels, but no one admitted knowing her. The other street women who might have seen her were protective. She was pretty, but too unskilled to be much of a threat to them. That might change, if she survived.

One brothel keeper told Laker that she thought Flavia might work a particular street, but Laker doubted she was telling the truth. She just wanted to be rid of him.

It took a long time to work out which women worked which street. What was left for newcomers was pretty poor. It was a matter of survival. Finally, a mixture of threats and bribes narrowed it down to a few possibilities.

It was late and cold when Hooper himself found her.

She was standing underneath the lamp on a narrow street, the mist already gathering in grey wraiths around the light itself, which reflected on the droplets collecting in her bright hair. She looked tired, and sad. But she was a handsome girl; perhaps her mother had once looked like that. She certainly had no resemblance whatsoever to Seth Marlowe.

She did not see him until he was almost within the arc of the light thrown by the lamp. She gave a slight start. He wondered if in her imagination she was somewhere else, warm and safe …

She turned round with an automatic flinch, then forced herself to smile. 'Looking for a little company, Mister?' Her expression was painfully bright.

Hooper felt as if he'd received a physical blow. How could any man bear to think of his own child doing this, even in desperation to survive? What should he do? How would she understand that what he wanted was to know the truth? Which might be colder than the winter night closing in.

'Truth is, I'm hungry,' he said. And it was the truth. 'Come and have a hot pie with me, in the pub around the corner, then we'll talk about what else.'

She looked at him dubiously. 'You want me to eat with you?' She spoke well, with no broad accent, but then if she were Marlowe's daughter, she had had a good education, at least until she ran away. If he forced Marlowe to show him the letters, he would know if it came from an educated hand, or not; if the grammar were correct, or deliberately aping ignorance. Was that one of the reasons why Marlowe would not show them to Celia?

'Yes,' he went on. 'I'm hungry. And I'd rather not eat alone.'

She pulled back. 'What do you want? You think you're not going to pay me?'

He took money out of his pocket and gave her two crowns. 'Enough to start with?' he asked.

She nodded and took the coins, looking at them carefully, then put them in a well-hidden pocket in her skirt. 'All right. I'll eat with you.'

He could see she was still suspicious, but she was hungry, too. He guessed she didn't often have a good meal, in a warm room. What in heaven's name had happened to her that she had chosen this life, instead of remaining with her father?

The wind was rising, and bitingly cold. He took her arm gently, and she allowed herself to be led towards the corner of the main road.

'What's your name?' he asked.

She hesitated for a moment, then jerked her chin up. 'Bessie,' she said, her voice suddenly harsher, as if it were strangled in her throat.

He was more certain than ever that this girl was Flavia, but he acted as if he believed her and kept his hand gently but firmly on her arm.

They turned the corner into the main street. The sign of the Dog and Duck was twenty yards ahead. She came willingly enough into the warm, brightly lit public house. He took a table and they sat, and then he ordered Irish stew for both of them. It came with rich gravy and plenty of meat and potatoes. It was not like the stew Celia made, but it was good all the same.

'Bessie,' he began. 'It's a nice name. I knew of a woman with hair exactly the colour of yours. Her name was Rose. She was married to a man who was very stiff and self-righteous, always telling everyone how they ought to behave.'

Flavia stiffened uncomfortably in her seat. 'Friend of yours, was he?' she asked suspiciously.

'No. Actually, I don't like him, but that's because he was very unkind to my wife. He accused her of writing anonymous letters to him.' He watched her closely now.

She flushed very slightly and took another spoonful of stew, looking away from him while she ate it. She did not ask what 'anonymous' meant.

He ate also; he really was hungry.

Finally, she looked up. 'What did you do?'

'Don't you want to know what it said?' He was curious what she would say.

'Something bad, I suppose.' She shrugged. 'Why are you talking to me?'

'I wondered when you would ask me that.' He did not answer the question. 'I didn't see the letters. And he didn't show them to my wife, just waved one around and said it was vile, and untrue. All lies. And he said that if she wrote another, he would tell everyone. And that she wasn't to see the young woman who is going to marry him, and who is her best friend.'

'Oh …' She looked confused, uncertain how she should react.

'Which upset her very much,' Hooper went on.

'Once she's married him, she's got to do as he tells her,' she said flatly. She was speaking of something she understood only too well.

'And if she doesn't?' he asked.

'He'll hit her. Husbands can do that. Where do you

come from, anyway? Not that it makes any difference, whoever you are.' She looked away for a moment. 'Very proper, was he? Friends with the vicar, and all?'

'Oh, I believe so. Vicars have to be friends with everyone, even if they don't like them very much. They have to try and see the best in people.'

She looked at him dismissively. 'Oh, yeah? Why would you say that to me? I'm just a ... girl off the street!' Suddenly she was angry and bitter, even close to sudden tears.

'All sorts of people lie, Flavia, and all sorts tell the truth.'

Her face was white. 'What did you call me?'

'Flavia. That's your name, isn't it?' he said gently.

The shock made her hunch into herself, as if he had threatened to shake her. She was quite obviously very frightened. Either she did not know what to say, or she was too terrified to speak at all.

'I think you are Flavia Marlowe,' he said softly. 'And Rose Marlowe was your mother. You don't seem to resemble him at all, but I think Seth Marlowe is your father.'

She did not deny it, but her eyes were filled with horror. 'I'm not going back!' She almost choked on her words.

'Of course you're not,' he promised. 'Is what's in the letters true? It certainly frightened him very badly.'

'Good! And of course it's true. I don't lie.'

'Lots of people don't lie, but we all make mistakes.'

She banged the spoon down in her dish and started to push back from the table, her face bleached white and full of fear. 'I'm not going …'

'You are not going anywhere you don't want to, Flavia.' Hooper stood up and caught her hand. 'But the letters have to stop, because other people are being blamed for them, and are going to be punished. You didn't mean that to happen, did you?'

'No, of course I didn't. What about that poor girl he's going to marry? What happens to her?' she demanded, her voice shaking. 'I saw what he did to my mother. He hasn't changed. He can't. He ordered her around. "Do that, do this, don't do that! You're doing it all wrong! Do it the way I tell you!" All the time. He will break his new wife, the very way he broke my mother.' She was glaring at him, tears running down her cheeks. 'She wasn't bad, like he said she was, my mum. She just wanted to laugh now and then, to look pretty. That's not a sin. She wasn't a tart or a whore. She just wanted to be happy … and not beaten!'

'We all do, Flavia,' he said gently. 'So, there's something broken inside him, not her.'

'There is now!' She was raising her voice, angry and desperate with pain. 'She took her own life. There's no forgiveness for that, 'cause you're dead and can't repent.'

'Did he say that?'

'They all say that!'

'And how do they know? Anyone ever come back from being dead and say so?' He heard his own voice with incredulity.

She stared at him.

'Sit down,' he told her softly. 'We don't need the whole pub listening to us.'

She obeyed. 'She did take her own life,' she said so quietly he had to lean forward across the table to hear her. 'After she lost the baby, she didn't seem to care any more. She just … we went to the seaside for the day. On the train. It's not far. In the evening, when the tide was going out, she went for a walk on the sand. And she just walked into the sea, and kept on walking. I called out to her, ran along the sand and got all wet, but she was too far away. She might have heard me, or maybe she didn't. But she just went on walking into the water, until it took her, and she couldn't get back. She didn't look back not even once. She wanted to go and leave us.'

The girl bent over and surrendered to her pain.

Hooper kneeled on the floor beside her and put his arm around her, holding her so she could lean against him and weep all the tears she had kept inside since that terrible night.

Nobody in the public house stared at them. They had all seen grief before, such loneliness and pain, and they understood.

Celia heard the front doorbell, and then the sound of the door closing. She froze. Who would ring, when they could get in anyway?

'Celia!' It was Hooper's voice.

She shot to her feet and opened the sitting-room door to the hall, and then stopped. Hooper was standing just inside the front door, and beside him was a young woman, very young, a girl, in fact. Celia judged that underneath the paint, she was probably well under twenty. Her dress was tight, too tight for modesty, even for flattery, and it was all too clearly well worn. But the most striking thing about her was a mass of thick, curling, auburn hair, loosely tied back and pinned up, but coming undone by the wind.

Then Celia noticed her face that, in spite of the rouge, was pretty: fine features, delicate bones, wide mouth.

Hooper spoke to the girl first. 'Flavia, this is my wife, Celia.' He looked at Celia and she knew what he was going to say. She was right. 'Celia, this is Flavia Marlowe, although I think she prefers not to use her last name.'

Celia met the girl's eyes and saw the fear and confusion in them, and also that she was embarrassed. The street life was not a choice, it was a means of survival in a world that confused her, the least awful of her choices, or perhaps it had seemed so at the beginning.

Celia smiled. 'Come in, you must be freezing. Would you like a cup of tea, perhaps cocoa?'

'Thank you. I ... I ...' Flavia hesitated, clearly not knowing what to say.

'Cocoa?' Celia suggested. 'Why don't you go and sit down by the fire, and I'll bring it in for you.' Without waiting for an answer, she opened the sitting-room door and then went into the kitchen.

She heated the milk, enough for all three of them, and stirred in the cocoa powder. Her mind raced with all the possibilities as to what might have happened. Hooper had obviously been looking for her, that much she knew – and successfully – but to what end? Did she know who had written the letters? Was it she herself? Did she say? And did Marlowe know it was her, which would be why he had not shown them to anyone else? Or had he only guessed?

But if he knew, why had he blamed Celia?

She remembered the sudden light in his face. That would explain it, if that had been the moment when he realised who had sent them: not her and not Arthur Roberson. Why had Hooper brought the girl here? Maybe not only to settle the matter, but for her own safety.

Celia filled three mugs, put them on a tray with a few oatmeal and chocolate biscuits, and carried it through to the sitting room.

As if back in childhood habit again, maybe with the familiarity of a home, pictures on the walls, winter flowers on the table, Flavia rose, took the tray from Celia and put it gently on the little table nearest the fire. She passed the first mug to Hooper, and took the second for herself, looking for somewhere to set it down again. She knew without being told that the chair she had been in was Celia's. She moved instead to one end of the sofa.

They sipped their cocoa in silence. Celia thought

they were probably all wondering how to approach the subject that must be in all of their minds. How much to say? It would be even worse to tiptoe around it, talking of everything else.

Celia felt the girl's eyes on her and wondered what she was feeling. Hatred for her father, or a longing for his approval? Even forgiveness? Grief for her mother? A need to have someone excuse Rose's suicide, find a reason why it was not the sin Marlowe had claimed it to be? Or did she wish that everyone would forget it, and take her for who she was, which was surely not a girl who willingly chose the streets as a way of life.

It was Hooper who broke the silence. He spoke directly to Celia, almost as if Flavia were not there. 'Have we got enough hot water for a bath? For Flavia?' he added quickly.

'Yes, of course,' Celia replied. 'Can't go to bed cold. She'd never sleep.'

While Flavia was soaking in the tub, Hooper spoke quietly to Celia in the sitting room.

'I'll go now and see Clementine. She needs to know that Flavia is with us and safe.'

'Good idea,' Celia agreed. 'And while you're there, please ask her if she has a dress that would suit a young girl. After all, tomorrow is Christmas Day.' She saw a look of amazement on his face. He had not been counting. She smiled. 'We're all ready, don't worry.'

After Hooper left and Flavia was preparing for bed, Celia said, 'You will stay with us over Christmas, won't you?'

Flavia looked puzzled and embarrassed, not knowing what to say, but she could not hide the longing in her face.

'Good,' Celia accepted, as if she had actually answered.

Flavia smiled shyly. Then a certain look of alarm came into her face, almost of terror.

Celia understood immediately. 'You don't need to go to church, if you don't wish to. I will go for all of us.'

Hooper pulled his heavy naval pea coat around him. The rising wind, cruel with the beginning of sleet on its edge, would probably turn to snow before morning. He put his head down and walked into the wind.

It was just short of three-quarters of a mile to the house where Clementine lodged. He could see the thin crack of light under the drawn curtains. He walked up to the door, lifted the brass lion's head knocker and let it fall. Within a few moments the door opened revealing Clementine standing in the hall. 'Mr Hooper!' she said in surprise.

He smiled. 'Good evening, Miss Appleby. I've come to ask a favour.'

'Please come in, it's a wretched night, and it's Christmas tomorrow.' She backed a little further and he closed the door and followed her, grateful for the enveloping warmth. 'What can I help with?' she asked.

He had already decided to tell her at least that he had found Seth Marlowe's daughter. She would know sooner or later, and he preferred to be open. 'I was looking for Seth's daughter,' he began. 'I found her. Brought her back to our home, because she had nowhere to go. She's on the streets, Clementine, just as Seth told us.'

She took a deep, shaky breath and nodded, realisation of all that that meant dawning in her face.

'She had nowhere to go,' he continued, 'so I took her there. I need to borrow a dress, if you have one you can spare. She needs it for tomorrow.' He saw her look of confusion. 'She needs something more … suitable,' he said gently. 'She was working … on the street. Looking for customers.' His voice wavered as he said it. It sounded like a judgement, and it was, but of Marlowe, not of his daughter.

She bit her lip. 'I was hoping her father was exaggerating,' she whispered. 'Is she … all right?' She was clearly struggling.

He decided to tell her as much of the truth as she would discover anyway. No, that was not honest: she would hear Seth Marlowe's side of the story. Hooper would tell her Flavia's.

'I don't think so,' he replied. 'She wrote the letters he received. Her hatred for him is very deep. And, if she believes what she is saying, I'm not surprised.' Briefly, choosing very few words, he told her what Flavia had told him. It was not until he finished that he realised how harsh it sounded. The understanding of it was in Clementine's face. It would be a lie if he tried to moderate it now, and she would know it.

'What are you going to do?' she asked softly. There was a very real fear in her eyes. Did she believe him, or was she already trying to think of a way in which it was not Seth's fault?

He hurt almost as much for her as for Flavia, perhaps because hers was a new wound, a fall rather than a crash from a greater height.

'I don't know,' he admitted. 'For now, she is warm and fed, and has somewhere to spend Christmas. She shouldn't be alone, certainly not on the street in this freezing weather. I think it's going to snow tonight.' That was irrelevant. The real bone-aching coldness was inside, and they both knew that.

'And after tomorrow?' Clementine whispered.

'I don't know,' he admitted again. 'But I can't send her back to the street.'

'Of course not,' she agreed. 'Perhaps … perhaps we can bring about a reconciliation? Seth often speaks of repentance and forgiveness.' Her face looked pinched with the struggle to hope, and the pain of knowledge that perhaps she was asking for a miracle. But he knew that she wanted to believe.

'Of course,' he agreed. What else could he say? They spoke a little longer, then he said good night and wished her a happy Christmas. He went out again into the bitter night, carrying the clothes that Clementine had lent: pretty clothes, suitable for a young woman.

While Hooper was making his way home, Celia was listening to Flavia struggling through her account of her life after her mother died and she herself had taken to a haphazard life on the streets, always hungry, often cold, but she swore it was better than returning to live with her father. It was clear that she was terrified of him.

'I did fight back once,' she said, looking up at Celia as if her belief in Flavia's courage mattered.

Celia found it painful to watch the girl struggle to maintain some dignity, and her need to tell somebody at last about her loneliness, fear, and then over-whelming grief.

'I watched her walk into the sea, without even looking back,' Flavia said, her eyes not moving from Celia's. 'I was on the beach. I ran up to the edge of the water without even feeling it, calling after her. But she wanted to go into the water, and the darkness, and not exist any more.' The tears were running down her face now.

Celia moved towards her. She had to think of something positive to say, anything at all. 'Maybe if he'd known, he would have tried to stop her. You don't know how sorry he could be now. Perhaps he just doesn't know how to say so. Some people don't.'

'He isn't sorry!' Flavia said with total conviction.

'You can't know that,' Celia started.

'Yes, I can. We were close to the long wharf that goes right out into the deep water, dragging anything under. I felt how strong it was when it was up to my knees.' She choked and control slipped away from her. 'I saw him! We'd gone, just the two of us, on to the beach and he had been looking for us, and found us. I saw him standing on the wharf, watching us … watching her die. He didn't do a thing. Not anything!' She looked at Celia's face. 'He just watched.'

There was nothing to say. Celia slipped forward on to her knees and took the girl in her arms, holding her more and more tightly, gently stroking her hair, and putting her cheek next to Flavia's, which was soft and warm, and wet with tears.

It was sometime later that she reached a decision. She must speak to Arthur Roberson, who was going to repeat his sermon on the gift of universal forgiveness brought back into the world by the birth of Christ. He had to change it. She did not know exactly what she would say to him, but she would say it this evening, while there was still time for him to change it. Tomorrow would be too late.

Celia slowly let go of the girl and sat back. 'I'm going to see the vicar.'

Flavia's eyes filled with fear. 'About me? You can't let me stay here because I'm a … I'm a bad woman?'

'What?' Celia was appalled. 'Great heavens, no!

You are welcome here as long as you like! But definitely for Christmas … and Boxing Day. And after. I want to tell him what he must say in his sermon. I know what he's planning to say, and it's wrong.'

'You tell him what to say?' Flavia was confused.

'Not usually,' said Celia, with a little smile. 'But I'm going to this time. He talked about forgiveness a few days ago.' It seemed like for ever since that Sunday.

'Don't you believe in forgiveness?' Flavia was confused, but she said it as if she urgently needed to know.

'Yes, I do. Of course, I do,' Celia answered. 'But I've got to explain something to him. Stay here. Keep warm. Put more coal on the fire when it needs it. But keep the guard up so nothing falls out and burns the carpet. And have more biscuits, if you would like. I'll be back.' She kissed the girl gently on the cheek, then went into the hall and put on her coat, and a scarf around her head and neck. Then she opened the door and went out quietly into the still-rising wind and the rain.

She walked quickly, reluctant to leave Flavia, but she could not have Arthur Roberson say with passion, on Christmas Day, when the whole village would be there, something he would bitterly regret. She must persuade him of it tonight, while there was still time for him to change it.

The dark path stretched ahead of her, deserted by everyone else. They would be home with their families, or else with their cats and dogs, sleeping to the crackle of flames, unaware of the power of the wind, or the ice on the edge of it. She pulled her scarf tighter and made her step a little faster.

Finally, she reached the vicarage and knocked on the door. Several minutes went by and she had to knock again before Arthur Roberson finally answered.

'Celia! Is something wrong?' He looked startled and almost immediately anxious. 'Come in! Come in! What's happened?'

She closed the door, having to push it shut against the wind, then followed him into his study, where the fire was roaring up the chimney.

'Oh dear,' Arthur said, regarding it. 'I rather overdid it.'

Celia did not say so, but she thought that it might be habit when he was alone. She, too, had needed more warmth, more life of a fire, when she had been by herself and it was dark and cold outside.

'What is wrong, my dear?' he said again.

'John has found Flavia, Marlowe's daughter,' she said, keeping it as brief as possible. 'She's at our house, and will stay there as long as she wishes.'

His face filled with joy. 'Seth will be delighted. I—'

'I doubt that,' she cut across him. 'She's all that he said of her, Arthur. She lives on the street as a prostitute. And he was right, Rose did take her own life.'

His face crumpled.

'It's worse than that, Arthur, much worse,' she said quietly, hating having to do it. 'He was so cruel that Rose would rather die than live with him any longer. She walked into the sea, until it took her and she couldn't come back.'

He shut his eyes and his face was filled with pain.

Celia had to finish it. 'Flavia told me she ran along the shore, calling after her mother, but Rose did not look back. She went into the darkness and the cold willingly.' Her throat was tight with the effort it took to continue. 'And that isn't all. Flavia saw Seth on the wharf above them, watching as well … and doing nothing.'

'Oh, sweet God!' he said in horror.

'She told me he saw her, and at first she was too paralysed with horror to fight him. But eventually she did. He tried to hold on to her, but she bit him and kicked him until he let go of her, and she ran away. A life on the streets was better than going back with him.'

She looked up at him. 'Arthur, when you speak tomorrow, speak about repentance and promise the forgiveness of God. But also remind us that it is useless, without understanding what you did that was wrong, and why it was wrong, ugly, painful, and it is not who you want to be ever again. Only then do you begin to heal, and gradually become a person who would never do that again. Then you can so easily be forgiven,' she went on, 'by anyone who cares at all for you. Because you are no longer the same person. Of course, you also have to forgive others. But you have seen ugliness, right inside yourself, and you understand how easy it is to make excuses, and how hard really to face the truth and change.' She took a deep breath. 'Then you forgive others as a deliberate act, and because you couldn't do anything else. In a sense, you are acknowledging your inner self.'

He searched for words, but did not find them. It

was clear in his face, and the hands knotted in front of him.

'Arthur, say it all! Repentance is no use without understanding, and then the real healing can begin! Change. Then God can't help but forgive you, and forget the sin, because it is no longer who you are!' She gazed at him steadily, willing him to understand, to turn around the simplicity of the forgiveness he had imagined in his mind, and instead accept her more complicated world, but one that seemed so much easier to believe.

'Blind, unconditional pardon doesn't heal, Arthur,' she went on. 'And we need to be healed. All of us, but Seth the most, if he really watched Rose walk into the sea because she wished to die, and saw Flavia desperate on the shore, crying out. He could have prevented her death, and all he did was watch. He may tell you he has repented, but he hasn't even understood the nature and the depth of those faults.'

Roberson struggled to find words, or perhaps it was to know what he wanted to say. 'He knows he has faults, Celia …' he started, then hesitated. 'Faults. You're right: if we can't look at them and name them, then it's not repentance.'

'We all have faults, Arthur,' she agreed. 'It's not

hard to admit that, and impossible to deny it. Naming them, the real ones that are shaming, ugly, revealing of your weaknesses, is quite another thing. That's embarrassing, even humiliating, but it means you see them, they're real. It's … owning the ugliness of them.' She stopped. She saw in his face that he needed time to grasp the difficulty of what she was saying, the enormity. And the truth. She remained silent and unmoving. She saw the moment when he believed it, like the slow dawning of a deeper radiance inside him. He did not even ask her how she knew it was the truth; it did not matter. He knew it now for himself.

'Thank you,' he said softly.

Before either of them could say anything more, there was a crash as the front door slammed open against the wall and the impact shivered all the way to the study. Arthur rose to his feet as Seth Marlowe flung open the study door. His face was twisted with fury, his eyes glaring. For a moment, he saw only Arthur Roberson. Then he saw Celia and the last vestige of control slipped from him. 'You interfering woman! How dare you bring my slut of a daughter here into this village, into my home? On the doorstep of my wife-to-be! Clementine has told me everything.'

Arthur held up his hand and stepped in front of Celia, as if to prevent Marlowe from physically attacking her. 'Be quiet, Seth, you're only making yourself ridiculous. It's time for the truth. Your wife walked into the sea, intending to die. And you did nothing.'

'How dare you?' Marlowe was shaking with rage, the veins standing out on his temples and his neck.

'And what is just as bad,' Roberson continued, 'perhaps even worse, was how your daughter, your child, ran along the shore crying out to her mother, and you still did nothing.'

'You know nothing about it, you interfering fool! I know people! I will have you thrown out, defrocked for breaking the seal of confession! You're finished ...'

Arthur shook his head. 'Seth, what is wrong with you? Have you no shame, man? No pity?'

'She betrayed me!' Marlowe snorted, his face, even the angles of his body, reflecting his fury. 'Rose took her own life! That is a sin for which you can't repent, because your time is finished by your own hand!'

'For God's sake, Seth! I'm not talking about Rose! God will take care of her, or your child, whom you abandoned. I'm talking about you: your sins, your arrogance, your cruelty to those most vulnerable, over and over again, week after week.'

'They're conspiring to poison Clementine against me!' Marlowe shouted back. 'Do you expect me to simply let them?' He drew breath to continue, but he was interrupted by the arrival of Hooper, who was standing in the study doorway, his arm around Clementine's shoulders.

Hooper looked at Clementine's face, expecting horror, and then pain. It was there, the realisation rather than amazement, or disbelief. Nevertheless, her eyes were full of tears. Something inside her was deeply wounded.

She turned to Seth Marlowe, no fear in her face, only pity. 'You are not sorry for what is really wrong, Seth. It is always everybody's fault but yours. And yet you have not forgiven them, because you have not forgiven yourself.' She took a deep breath. 'I thought I loved you, and I so desperately wanted to belong, to be part of a family, to have children.'

Marlowe's face was contorted with rage and confusion. 'How dare you?' he shouted, but he choked on the last word. He looked around the room: at Clementine, who stared back at him unflinchingly;

at Arthur Roberson, who had moved up beside her and put one hand gently on her arm. And then at Hooper, who appeared immovable, both physically and emotionally.

'You have no place here, Seth,' Arthur said quietly. 'Unless and until you accept humility, and above all, the gentleness of heart to forgive.'

'Never!' Marlowe said furiously. He spun round and glared at Celia, then at Hooper. 'Go to hell, all of you!' And then he turned on his heel and stormed out. There was, for a moment, the roar of the rising wind, and then the crash of the front door slamming shut behind him.

There was a moment's silence; Hooper turned to Celia.

She knew what he was going to say. The same thought had occurred to her. 'Yes,' she said, before he could speak. 'Get Flavia. She mustn't be alone in the house, if he goes there. He's enraged enough to smash a window to get in.'

'Yes,' Roberson agreed. 'We'll lock the door behind you, but I don't think he'll come back here. We'll be fine.'

No one protested. No one denied the danger.

Hooper put on his coat and scarf, glanced at Celia

once more with a brief softening in his eyes, then went out. Roberson closed the door behind him and shot home the heavy bolts.

There was a moment's silence, then Celia spoke. 'Arthur, have you enough milk and cocoa to make hot drinks? They'll be frozen stiff when they get back.'

He looked at Clementine and smiled tenderly. 'Of course we have cocoa; it's required in every vicarage. And there's brandy, too.'

'Thank you,' Celia said, meeting his eyes in a moment of gratitude. Then she turned to Clementine and put her arm around her. 'Come and help me,' she invited.

Clementine leaned into her. 'Yes, of course.' As if slowly coming back to life, she asked, 'Do you know where everything is? Show me ...'

They went together and set about the task. They did not speak. It was a silent companionship, but Celia kept glancing at the younger woman whose world had just been so hideously shattered, and saw in her face a slight understanding of what she had lost, and that it had never really existed.

When Hooper returned with Flavia, the door was unbarred for them and they came inside. Clementine stared at Flavia with disbelief, then a slow radiant smile spread across her face. 'Bessie? Flavia …?'

As Flavia's fears dissolved, her body relaxed. Her eyes shone with amazement and relief. 'You … I?' She was lost for words.

Clémentine stepped forward, put her arms around the girl and held her close.

Roberson's smile grew wider and wider.

And then, quite suddenly, clear and pure, came the sound of church bells pealing a carol of joy into the night. It was calling them to the midnight service that heralded Christmas morning.

We hope you have enjoyed reading Anne Perry's
enthralling festive mystery.

Don't miss her other Christmas novellas,
as well as her many bestselling crime novels . . .

DISCOVER FESTIVE MYSTERIES
FROM THE INIMITABLE
ANNE PERRY

DON'T MISS ANNE PERRY'S LATEST THRILLERS
OF ESPIONAGE AND MURDER SET BETWEEN
THE WORLD WARS,
THE ELENA STANDISH SERIES

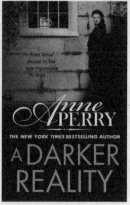

AND A NEW GENERATION OF PITT NOVELS,
FEATURING THOMAS'S BARRISTER SON, DANIEL,
IN THE DANIEL PITT SERIES

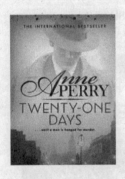

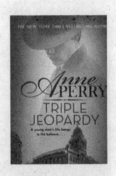

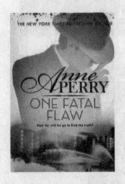

FOR MORE FROM ANNE PERRY, TRY
THE THOMAS PITT SERIES

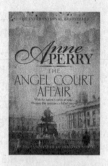

———————

BETHLEHEM ROAD
HIGHGATE RISE
BELGRAVE SQUARE
FARRIERS' LANE
THE HYDE PARK HEADSMAN
TRAITORS GATE
PENTECOST ALLEY
ASHWORTH HALL
BRUNSWICK GARDENS

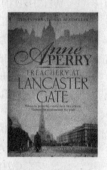

BEDFORD SQUARE
HALF MOON STREET
THE WHITECHAPEL CONSPIRACY
SOUTHAMPTON ROW
SEVEN DIALS
LONG SPOON LANE
BUCKINGHAM PALACE GARDENS
BETRAYAL AT LISSON GROVE
DORCHESTER TERRACE
MIDNIGHT AT MARBLE ARCH
DEATH ON BLACKHEATH
THE ANGEL COURT AFFAIR
TREACHERY AT LANCASTER GATE
MURDER ON THE SERPENTINE

———————

GO TO WWW.ANNEPERRY.CO.UK
TO FIND OUT MORE

DISCOVER THE
WILLIAM MONK SERIES

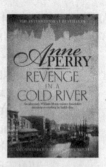

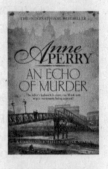

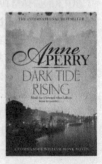

GO TO WWW.ANNEPERRY.CO.UK
TO FIND OUT MORE

THRILLINGLY GOOD BOOKS FROM CRIMINALLY GOOD WRITERS

CRIME FILES BRINGS YOU THE LATEST RELEASES FROM TOP CRIME AND THRILLER AUTHORS.

GN UP ONLINE FOR OUR MONTHLY NEWSLETTER AND BE THE FIRS^T TO KNOW ABOUT OUR COMPETITIONS, NEW BOOKS AND MORE.